"Why do you care wha

"Because your opinion matters to me, Dee. So what you think of the place that made me who I am matters to me, too."

"Why?" Dee's voice was barely more than a whisper. There was a hunger in her gaze that Tripp knew well. One he'd promised himself he wouldn't give in to.

"Because I like you, Dionna. A lot." The words scraped at Tripp's throat like tiny shards of glass.

"What if I said I like you, too, Tripp?"

Tripp's gaze dropped to her full lips. His brain was suddenly overwhelmed with imagining the taste and feel of those lush lips.

Tripp closed the space between them, his lips crashing into Dee's. One arm glided around her waist, tugging her against him, his body now pressed to hers. The other hand cradled her cheek, angling Dee's head as his lips glided over hers.

* * *

A Cowboy Kind of Thing
by Reese Ryan is part of the
Texas Cattleman's Club: The Wedding series.

Dear Reader,

When I was first invited to participate in the long-running Texas Cattleman's Club series, I was honored yet apprehensive about joining the list of fabulous authors who've made TCC a reader favorite. But writing Tessa Noble and Ryan Bateman's steamy friends-to-lovers story was pure joy.

I pushed the envelope a bit in *His Until Midnight*. Readers still talk about that standing desk scene in the barn. LOL! Tessa's brother, Tripp, also made an impression. Readers wanted his story, and I wanted to write it. And because reader Kim Matlock kept asking for it, in this book we finally get Tripp Noble's story.

I loved writing the push and pull between Tripp and Dionna, and watching their mutual attraction blossom into something deeper. Collaborating with LaQuette, Karen Booth, Joanne Rock, Nadine Gonzalez and Jessica Lemmon—authors whose work I adore— made this project even more fun.

Thank you for joining us for the passion and drama of The Wedding. For book news, giveaways and more, visit ReeseRyan.com/DesireReaders and join my VIP Readers newsletter list and private VIP Reader group.

Until our next adventure!

Reese Ryan

REESE RYAN

A COWBOY KIND OF THING

Special thanks and acknowledgment are given
to Reese Ryan for her contribution to the
Texas Cattleman's Club: The Wedding miniseries.

Recycling programs
for this product may
not exist in your area.

ISBN-13: 978-1-335-58163-1

A Cowboy Kind of Thing

Harlequin Enterprises ULC
22 Adelaide St. West, 41st Floor
Toronto, Ontario M5H 4E3, Canada
www.Harlequin.com

Printed in U.S.A.

Reese Ryan writes sexy, emotional love stories with family drama, career dilemmas and a cast of complicated characters.

Connect with Reese, award-winning author of the fan-favorite Bourbon Brothers series, @ReeseRyanWrites via Facebook, Twitter, Instagram or TikTok, or at ReeseRyan.com. Join her VIP Readers Lounge at http://bit.ly/VIPReadersLounge. Check out her YouTube show where she chats with fellow authors at https://bit.ly/ReeseRyanChannel.

Books by Reese Ryan

Harlequin Desire

The Bourbon Brothers

Savannah's Secrets
The Billionaire's Legacy
Engaging the Enemy
A Reunion of Rivals
Waking Up Married
The Bad Boy Experiment

Valentine Vineyards

A Valentine for Christmas

Texas Cattleman's Club: The Wedding

A Cowboy Kind of Thing

Visit the Author Profile page
at Harlequin.com for more titles.

You can also find Reese Ryan on Facebook,
along with other Harlequin Desire authors,
at Facebook.com/HarlequinDesireAuthors!

To Kim Matlock, whose quiet determination birthed this miniseries. And to K. Sterling—thank you for your continued support and generous spirit.

One

"What do you mean you aren't coming?"

Dionna Reed paced the floor of her hotel room at The Bellamy resort in Royal, Texas, where she'd arrived little more than an hour ago. She'd been expecting her best friend, actress Ariana Ramos, to arrive at the hotel any minute. Instead, her friend video called her to break the news that she wouldn't be coming to Royal after all.

"But this is *your* wedding, Ari. How can you *not* be here?" Dionna realized that her voice had risen higher than necessary. She didn't care. This was a full-out emergency.

"I've been dreaming about my wedding since I was five years old. Do you really think I'd prefer to be stuck here on set in Peru for another four weeks?" There was a slight tremble in Ari's voice, and instantly Dee felt guilty.

Yes, she'd sacrificed four days of her busy life to come to Royal—the hometown of Ari's fiancé, best-selling author Xavier Noble. But she was supposed to be there to lend moral support and her honest opinion as Ariana and her fiancé worked with their wedding planner to make arrangements for their nuptials.

Forget about yourself for a minute. Think of how devastating this must be for her.

"I'm sorry, Ari. I know how much you were looking forward to this." Dionna settled onto the brown leather sofa as she surveyed the luxury two-bedroom hotel suite her friend had probably laid out a small mint for. "What happened exactly?"

"We were four hours away from the film wrap-up party when the bomb dropped," Ari said, anger rising in her voice. "You know how I said my costar, Nicholas Rainey, gives me the creeps because of the way he's always looking at me when the camera isn't rolling… Well, apparently my spider-senses are on point. It seems Nick's eye isn't the only thing that has been roaming."

"Don't tell me…"

"Yes!" Ari hissed. "*Multiple* women have made harassment claims against the creep. Since the first woman filed a suit against him five days ago, at least ten other women have come forward—including his sister-in-law!"

"Oh no. Isn't his wife pregnant with their third or fourth kid right now?" Dionna asked.

"Their fifth!" Ari practically screeched.

"Wow. This dude is absolute trash," Dionna said. "But the studio has already wrapped up filming. What do they plan to do? Shelve the film and hope the fury dies down?"

"They're taking these claims seriously, and they should. Nick's agent and PR firm have already dropped him like a radioactive rock, and the studio is yanking him from the film. I support the decision one hundred percent. But that means we're going to have to reshoot *every freaking scene* that handsy jerk was in. And since he was the leading man, we're practically reshooting the entire film."

"I'm so sorry, Ari. And I'll do whatever I can to help. Should I call the wedding planner and try to get this rescheduled?" Dionna reached into her leather WANT Les Essentiels vertical tote bag and pulled out her planner.

"No! Don't!"

"Why not?" Dionna surveyed the current date. "This is supposed to be an exploratory trip to make decisions about your wedding. Seems pretty important for the bride to be here."

"We've already rescheduled twice. We can't afford to put this off any longer."

"But the wedding isn't until June," Dionna reminded her.

"And it's already the end of February. Not much lead time in the wedding industry. We've pushed this as far back as we can. I *cannot* cancel these meetings again. They must go on as planned," Ari insisted.

"Without the bride?" Dionna asked incredulously. "Is Xavier going to video call you to make every single decision?"

"About that…" Ari's expression reminded Dee of Lucille Ball's whenever she had to deliver bad news to her best friend, Ethel Mertz, on *I Love Lucy*.

"There's more bad news?"

"Ex won't be there either," Ari said sheepishly.

"Why? This is *his* hometown. *He's* the one who wanted to get married here instead of in LA." Dionna was still miffed that Ari had broken tradition and moved the wedding to the groom's hometown instead of hers.

But where they got married actually mattered to Ex, whereas Ari's only concern was that their wedding be spectacular. Ari considered moving the wedding a peace offering to Xavier's family who seemed less than thrilled about their son marrying into Hollywood. A small sacrifice for the man she adored.

It was sweet, sure. But it made planning the wedding complicated. Especially now.

"I know, sweetie," Ari cooed, employing the same voice she'd used to talk Dee into questionable decisions since the two of them had met and become best friends in middle school. "But the European book tour for *The Silence* is going really well. Xavier's publisher wants to extend the tour and they've lined up several talk show appearances."

"But this has been planned for weeks," Dee said.

"Which is why he'd intended to turn them down. But now that I'm not able to make the trip, we thought he might as well ride this wave while the book is hot. You know how fickle our industries can be, Dee. I need you there. No one knows me better than you. You always know exactly what I'm thinking before I've said a word. You know what I like and what I don't. You're the perfect stand-in for me. I even trust you to handle the tasting menu. If I need to make tweaks later, I can. But at least we'll get things started."

Dionna tapped the end of her fountain pen against her planner as she mulled over her friend's words.

"I *really* need your help on this, Dee," Ari said. "There's no one else in the world I'd trust to do this. Not even Sasha," she said of her younger sister. "Pretty please. I'll even let you pick your own maid-of-honor dress."

That got Dionna's attention. She had been terrified her friend would put her in a sleeveless, backless dress that bared her navel.

"Deal," Dee said before Ari could change her mind.

"Thanks, Dee. You're the best friend a girl could ask for."

"Let's see if you still think that after the wedding. Because while I do know you like the back of my hand, I can't say the same for your fiancé."

Ari grinned a little too wide. "Don't worry, babe. Got that covered."

Dionna groaned, not liking the mischievous twinkle in her best friend's eyes.

"You're really backing out of this thing?" Tripp Noble asked his cousin Xavier as he pulled out of the driveway of The Noble Spur—the ranch Tripp's family owned and had run for four generations. "You're not getting cold feet about the wedding, are you? You can be straight with me."

Tripp and Ex had been thick as thieves as mischievous boys growing up on The Noble Spur together. But Ex had left Royal long ago. He'd dreamed of being a famous author—and he'd done just that. In fact, he'd become more successful than either of them could've dreamed.

Xavier had lived all over the country and currently called Los Angeles home. Yet, the two of them remained close. Still, it'd been a while since they'd seen each other in person. So Tripp had been looking forward to spending time with his cousin.

"No, I don't have cold feet. Are you kidding me? Ariana is the best thing that's ever happened to me. I can't wait to marry her," Ex said without hesitation.

"Then why are you *really* bailing on this trip home?"

"I told you why. My publisher wants to extend the tour." Ex sounded a little too defensive.

"And…"

They might've spent the past decade or so apart, but Tripp still knew his cousin well.

"All right, you've got me," Xavier sighed. "Everything I said about the tour is true. But Ari has already made such a *huge* sacrifice in moving the wedding to Royal. I don't want to screw this up. This wedding needs to be everything Ari has ever wanted and more."

"Well, who would know what she wants better than you?"

"I know a lot about Ari," Ex said. "But when it comes to this wedding stuff, I'm at a total loss. I cannot fuck this up. It's too important to her."

"Okay, so what's the plan? You rescheduling again?"

"Ari doesn't think we should. She wants to forge ahead and let Dionna handle the decision-making," Ex said.

"I realize they're close, but is Ariana really good with letting her bestie make decisions about her wedding?" Tripp asked.

He'd only met his cousin's future bride via video calls. But he couldn't imagine she'd want to be hands-off for something as important as her own wedding.

"Ari insists no one knows her better, and I'd have to agree."

"What about what *you* want?" Tripp asked. "I get that she's already conceded on the location. But you're telling me you don't want to have any other input into the ceremony? I mean, assuming this is going to be your only wedding—"

"Ha ha ha," Ex said drolly. "You're so un-fucking-funny."

"I'm just saying, if you're only planning to do this once, I'd think you'd want your stamp on things in at least some way," Tripp said.

"Glad you mentioned it. That's where you come in."

"Say what?" Tripp took his eyes off the road for a nanosecond and had to jam his foot on the brakes so he wouldn't hit a squirrel that darted across the street.

"Dionna is filling in for Ari, and I'd like you to fill in for me. You know me, Tripp. You know what I'd like, what I'd just roll with if it makes Ari happy, and what I'd hate."

"Dude. When it comes to the bachelor party, I got you. But what about me says *wedding planner*?"

"We've already hired a wedding planner, Rylee Meadows. She's flying into Royal this weekend." He could hear the grin in Xavier's voice. "All I'm asking is that you and Dionna work with her to ensure that this wedding has Ari's and my stamp on it. You know I wouldn't ask a favor this big if I didn't really need you."

Tripp sat in his truck, idling at a traffic light, and debated his cousin's request.

Of course, he was going to help Ex. They were blood and as close as brothers. So he'd do just about anything to help his cousin. Apparently even becoming a junior wedding planner.

Besides, hadn't he already been doing that the past couple of months by tossing around ideas about when and where the couple would get married?

Ariana recognized how important family was to Ex. So she'd roped Tripp into the phone chats about their wedding, and it had been his teasing-not-teasing comment about his aunt and uncle, Xavier's parents, being none too happy about the wedding being in LA that had prompted Ari to move the wedding to Royal.

He honestly hadn't expected her to give up her dream wedding location in LA. But it was evident that she loved his cousin, and he respected that. So he wanted this wedding to be amazing for Ari and Ex because they both deserved it.

If Ari could make such a huge sacrifice for Xavier, it wouldn't kill him to dedicate a few days to the cause.

"Okay, I'm in. Just tell me what you need," Tripp conceded.

"We were supposed to take the girls to dinner tonight. Show them why Royal is such a great place. Dionna is already in town, and to be honest, she isn't on board with having the wedding in Royal. I'd appreciate anything you could do to change her mind."

In their video chats, Ari's best friend was pretty, quiet and very by the book. With her tortoiseshell eyeglasses and her hair always pulled up, she'd given him hot librarian vibes. By the third call, she'd gotten a little more comfortable with him and loosened up a little. The two of them couldn't be more different, but there was something about Dee that Tripp liked.

"So you want me to show Dee a good time? Consider it done."

"I don't like the sound of that," Ex said.

"You asked me to change her mind about Royal." Tripp laughed.

"Dude, do *not* fuck this up for me. Ariana means *everything* to me, and Dee and Ari are closer than sisters."

"C'mon, man. You're in there like swimwear," Tripp teased. "Seriously, Ari adores you. You're good."

"She won't if my playboy cousin hooks up with her best friend and breaks her heart. I've seen marriages

crumble for a hell of a lot less. So excuse me if I don't
want to risk finding out how forgiving she'd be about
it," Xavier said in his serious voice.

Tripp was tempted to remind his cousin they were
talking about a grown-ass woman in her midthirties,
not some wide-eyed college coed. But Xavier didn't
seem inclined to debate the point, so Tripp let it go.
After all, it wasn't like he planned on hooking up
with Dee.

"I promise to be on my best behavior. *There*. Feel
better?" Tripp asked as he pulled into the lot of Corryna
Lawson's flower shop, Royal Blooms.

"Actually, I do." Xavier heaved a sigh. "Seriously,
thanks for doing this. I know wedding planning isn't
exactly in your wheelhouse."

"Just remember, you owe me one. Now, I have shit
to do, so I've gotta go. Hit me up when you get back
from the tour."

"Will do." Xavier ended the call.

Tripp parked his truck in the lot of the flower shop
and sighed. He honestly didn't have designs on Dionna. But the woman was as alluring as she was maddening. He'd be lying if he said the thought hadn't
crossed his mind.

Two

"You want me to work with Tripp on your wedding," Dee repeated her best friend's sheepish request. "This just keeps getting better."

"Tripp knows Ex as well as you know me. You're the perfect partners for this. And if there's anything pressing, you can always contact one of us. We'll get back to you as soon as we can," Ariana said.

"Do we really need to involve Tripp? I mean… I'm sure Rylee and I can work things out on our own."

"What's wrong with Tripp?" Ari asked. "He's handsome. He's hot. He's got a sense of humor."

"Exactly!" Dionna said. "He strikes me as the pampered playboy-type who has had everything in life handed to him. The kind of guy who doesn't take anything seriously. You realize that's the worst pos-

sible personality type you could match me up with…
on this project," she quickly clarified.

The last thing she wanted to do was give her friend
ideas. Ari had already hinted more than once that the
four of them should go on a double date.

"You're not being fair, Dee. Tripp is a rancher, and
from what I understand, he works as hard as any of
their ranch hands. And your opposing personalities
are what make you a great planning match. You'll
balance each other out. You'll make sure he's taking
this seriously, and he'll help you loosen up a little.
This is a celebration after all. I just want it to be the
best, most lavish one that little town has ever seen."

"Great. No pressure then," Dionna groused.

"Nothing you can't handle," Ariana assured her.
"Now, let's see what you're wearing to dinner."

"This *is* what I'm wearing to dinner." Dionna
glanced down at her white button-down blouse, black
pants and sensible shoes.

"Seriously?" Ari peered through the screen with
concern.

"This isn't a date," Dionna reminded her best friend.
"I'm meeting with the best man to iron out a few wedding details."

"It *is* a dinner date," Ariana objected after a suspi-
ciously pregnant pause. "I have to run, but wear something fun tonight and try to relax. Or else you two will
get off to a bad start."

Tripp Noble.

Just the thought of his handsome face, broad smile and those mesmerizing golden-brown eyes sent a shiver down her spine.

Do not fall for the trap, girl.

Yes, the man was handsome, funny and wealthy. But he could also be stubborn and incredibly frustrating, as he'd been on several of their video calls about the wedding over the past few months. One moment she'd fantasize about kissing Tripp's luscious lips. The next she'd want to wrap her hands around that thick neck of his and squeeze because he was so obstinate.

Sure, Tripp was attractive. Charming. Maybe even the slightest bit tempting. And he'd flirted with her a bit. But they were just too different. Besides, flirting was as second nature to a charismatic pretty boy like Tripp as breathing. It didn't mean he actually liked her.

Tripp had probably dated half the women who'd come through Royal. Dee had no intention of adding her name to that list.

She was thirty-five now. When she got involved again, it would be someone she could build a future with. Not another charmer who'd happily have the words *Eternal Bachelor* etched into his gravestone.

There was a knock at the door. "Delivery for Dionna Reed."

Dionna peeked through the peephole, trying to determine if the man outside her door was an actual hotel employee or a character in the opening scene of a murder mystery where she'd play the unwitting murder victim who'd been too stupid to live.

"Delivery from your bestie, Ari," the man said after knocking again.

Dionna undid the locks and opened the door cautiously. "I'm Dionna Reed."

"The instructions said you wouldn't open the door unless I said that last part," the man chuckled. "Guess your bestie knows you pretty well after all."

She frowned at the man. "You said you had a delivery?"

He straightened his expression and extended a box to her. She signed for it and tipped the man.

"What have you gotten me into this time, Ari?" Dee whispered to herself as she opened the gold box wrapped with a black-and-cream bow—the colors her best friend had chosen for her wedding.

Dionna pulled the garments from the box one at a time. Pretty, colorful skirts, blouses and dress pants. A textured, long-sleeved black minidress. A tangerine-colored one-shoulder midi dress. A pretty wrap minidress in a bold geometric print. A Mediterranean blue Kay Unger jumpsuit with a jacquard-print top and overlay skirt that went over midnight-blue crepe pants. And corresponding shoes and accessories for each outfit. All of it from Dee's very own closet.

Ari had been in Peru for weeks. When had her friend dug out the clothing Dee had purchased during their post-breakup retail therapy sessions and sent them to the hotel? She hadn't. It had to have been Ari's younger sister, Sasha.

She and Ari really needed to review when it was appropriate to use her emergency spare house key.

Her phone buzzed with a text message.

I see the package arrived. Your legs are amazing. I'd go with the black mini and lose the bun. Don't forget to send pics!

Ari Ramos didn't miss a single thing.

Dee sighed, then hung up each item of clothing.

After her two-year-long relationship had gone down in flames, she'd subconsciously adopted a black-and-white color scheme. The colors perfectly conveyed her constant mood: a combination of misery and hopefulness. But if her best friend had put this much effort into her look for this trip, maybe she should, too.

Hopefully, there were no more surprises in store for her tonight. She was nervous enough about meeting the frustrating yet intriguing Tripp Noble in the flesh.

Tripp parked his truck in front of The Bellamy and climbed out, clutching a glass vase overflowing with pink Asiatic lilies and pink, white and red roses. He handed his keys to the valet and made his way inside.

He and Dionna were supposed to meet at The Silver Saddle bar and tapas restaurant on the first floor of the luxury resort. But that was before he realized he'd be half an hour early, toting an oversized vase of flowers half as tall as he was.

It'd be awkward to sit at the tapas bar with that

huge bouquet on the table between them. So he'd deliver it to her hotel suite and they could go down to the restaurant together. He retrieved his cell phone from his back pocket, scrolled to Ariana's last group text update and noted Dee's room number. He made his way onto the elevator and leaned against the wall, grateful for a moment alone.

The seconds he spent watching the elevator numbers climb felt like the first moments of stillness he'd had all week. He'd pushed through the series of daily and weekly tasks essential to keeping his family's ranch—The Noble Spur—running so he could clear his schedule to spend time with his cousin and his fiancée. But now he'd be spending that time with Dionna instead.

They had four days to meet with vendors on Xavier and Ariana's behalf and get a good start on the decisions for their wedding, working with wedding planner Rylee Meadows.

After months of text messages and video chats, Tripp was still undecided about Dionna.

She was smart and savvy. But she was also a perfectionist who seemed determined to drain every ounce of fun out of the wedding planning process. She was also kind of a smart-ass. They often disagreed during their video chats. Dee had the kind of dry sense of humor Tripp had never really appreciated. Yet, he often found himself in a deep belly laugh about the conversations they'd had days or even weeks ago. There was just something about the woman that both got under his skin and made him wonder about the taste of hers.

Tripp shook the thought from his head, reminding himself of his promise to his cousin.

It wasn't as if he had some grand plan to ravish Dionna. Yes, they were friendly. And yes, there may have been some flirting on his part. But it had been more of a strategic move. An attempt to persuade her to agree with him. Not the precursor to some torrid affair. Still, the fact that Dionna was now off-limits made the idea of getting involved with her that much more tempting. In fact, he'd been slightly obsessed with the idea in the hours since he'd promised *not* to hook up with her. But that was just the rebel in him.

He'd get over it. They'd keep things friendly. And in a few days, Dee would be on her way. She'd go back to Hollywood where she belonged, and he'd go back to his life here in Royal. No harm, no foul.

So why was his pulse racing like a hormone-filled adolescent on his first date?

Tripp shut his eyes and released all the disquieting thoughts that had taken up residence in his head on the drive over. Then he knocked on Dee's hotel door.

Footsteps trailed to the door and there was a quiet pause as she likely checked the peephole. The door swung open.

"And what is this? The *I'm sorry for being a pushy nuisance* bouquet?"

Tripp shifted the flowers, which had inadvertently hidden his face. He studied her as she stood in the doorway with one hand propped on her generous hip.

Damn.

He knew Dionna was a beautiful woman. But he hadn't realized she was blessed with the kind of curves that sent his pulse into overdrive and made him a little weak at the knees. His mouth fell open, but his brain had temporarily forgotten how to make words.

"Tripp?" Dee's eyes widened with recognition. She pressed a hand to her cheek. "I'm sorry. I didn't realize it was you. When I looked through the peephole, all I saw was flowers. I thought it was another surprise delivery from Ariana to make up for not being here."

"Sorry to disappoint." Tripp shifted the vase. "Mind if I put these down?"

Dee stepped aside and gestured for Tripp to enter. "Those aren't for me, are they?" She studied the bouquet.

"You don't like them?" Tripp set the heavy crystal vase on the coffee table in the luxury hotel suite and rearranged a few of the stems that had gotten smushed on the journey.

"No. I mean, *yes*, I love the flowers. It's a beautiful arrangement. But this isn't a date, and no one has ever brought me flowers for a business dinner before."

Dee raised her hands to her face, as if to push her ever-present glasses up the bridge of her nose. Only, she wasn't wearing them. And for the first time, he really noticed how lovely her dark brown eyes were, highlighted by the drama of smoky, charcoal gray eye shadow and cat-eye eyeliner. Dee tugged her hair over one shoulder instead.

"Your hair..." Tripp said, before he could stop himself from thinking aloud, something his sister often admonished him about.

Just because you're thinking it, Tripp, doesn't mean you have to say it.

"What about it?" Dee ran her fingers through her sable-brown shoulder-length hair worn in loose twists rather than her signature sleek bun. "I had it up earlier. Maybe I should…"

"I like it. A lot," Tripp said. "I just haven't ever seen you without your glasses or with your hair down. You look *really* nice. Not that you don't normally," he added quickly.

Why am I blathering like an idiot?

"Thank you." Dee smoothed her palms down the fabric of the black minidress that molded to her curvy figure and showed off her thick brown thighs. Heat practically radiated off her cheeks as she flashed a lopsided smile. "But you didn't answer the question. Did you bring these for me?"

The way her eyes searched his filled his chest with an unsettling warmth.

"*Yes*, I brought them for you." Tripp shoved his hands into the pockets of his gray-and-black plaid pants. "But bringing them to you was actually Corryna Lawson's idea."

"Corryna?" Dionna's eyebrows scrunched as she rested her chin on her fist, the other arm folded across her body. "The name sounds familiar."

"She's the local florist I was telling you all about. The one you were convinced wouldn't cut it." Tripp tried to rein in a smirk. "The one I told you would be perfect for Ex and Ari's wedding."

"I see." Dee scrutinized the flower arrangement more critically as she turned the vase and rearranged a few of the stems. "While this is certainly a lovely arrangement, I'll need to see more before we commit to anything."

"Of course." Tripp tried his best not to break into a full victory grin as the two of them stood there. An awkward silence filled the space.

"Sorry about the way I answered the door," she said, finally. "It's made this weirder and more awkward than it should be." Dionna ran her fingers through her twists again and flashed a nervous smile. "It's good to finally meet you, Tripp."

She extended her hand in a handshake while he extended his arms for a hug. Then she opened her arms to give him a hug, but he'd extended his hand for a handshake. They both laughed nervously and ended up sharing an awkward hug.

What was it about this woman that made him revert to his floundering teenage self? Before he'd discovered the disarming power of the Noble family charm and his signature smile?

"It's good to finally meet you, too, Dionna." Tripp released her, quietly inhaling her subtle scent, like a field of wildflowers wafting on a calm spring breeze. "But I feel like we already know each other."

Dee folded her arms and raised one brow. "True. You're the handsome town flirt who enjoys flying by the seat of his pants."

"And you're Ms. Do-It-by-the-Book, let's get all of our ducks in a row before we move forward." He said the last part in his best mock Dionna voice.

Dionna burst into laughter. A wide grin spread across her face, her dark eyes sparkling. She poked him in the ribs. "I do *not* sound like that, Austin Charles Noble the *third*." She stressed the suffix.

"Oh, we're going straight to my government name, huh?" He chuckled, then pointed a finger at her. "Don't make me regret telling you that."

Dionna shrugged and gave him an innocent "Who me?" smile before laughing again. A sound he was already obsessed with.

He'd loved her unique laugh from the first time he'd heard it in a video call. It'd been a notable contrast to her serious nature. But in person, the sound was so light and pure. He couldn't help smiling.

"So are we going to eat or not? Because the last thing I ate was that sad meal they served on the plane, and I'm starving." Dee pressed a hand to her belly.

"Absolutely!" Tripp gestured toward the door. "Whenever you're ready."

"Great. I just need to grab my wedding notebook and a few of the samples I brought that will give us a better sense of what Ari and Ex want for the wedding."

"Slow your roll, Dee." Tripp put a hand on her shoulder, pinning her in place. "You just arrived. I've had a really long day, and you probably have, too. How about if tonight we just relax, have a little fun, and get to know each other better? We can go all in with the wedding stuff when we meet with Rylee to-morrow."

Dee stared at him in silence as she worried her lower lip with her teeth. "Okay... But it's not—"

"A date," Tripp finished, trying not to be insulted by her insistence on it not being a date when she smelled like spring and looked good enough to eat. "I think we're both clear on that."

His mind was. His body... Not so much.

Three

Dionna reached for her oversized WANT Les Essentiels tote bag. But the size of the bag made the length of the dress seem much smaller by comparison. And she was already self-conscious about the amount of thigh showing.

Dee nibbled on her lower lip and glanced up at Tripp who was gazing at her with a look that fell somewhere between a bemused child and a voracious wolf. She sighed quietly.

What would Ariana do?

Dionna reached into her bag and grabbed the black Vavvoune Ursa wristlet wallet her best friend had given her for her birthday. She slipped her cell phone inside the zippered pouch, then slipped the strap over her wrist.

The restaurant was downstairs, so she wouldn't need a coat.

Dee raked her fingers through her hair, unaccustomed to her loose hair brushing her shoulders. "Ready."

Tripp opened the door and she stepped into the carpeted hallway. She'd requested a room far from the elevator because it would be quieter. Now she regretted that choice. Because it meant walking in awkward silence beside Tripp who was taller and even more handsome than he'd appeared in their video chats.

Plus, he smelled divine. A combination of citrus, ginger and clean laundry fresh out the dryer. She had the sudden urge to wrap herself up like a burrito in a blanket draped with that scent. She'd sleep like a baby, something she didn't often do.

At the end of the hallway, she veered toward the right. But Tripp hooked his large hand around her waist and steered her left.

"Elevator is this way," Tripp said in response to her startled look.

"I'm pretty sure it's this way." Dee jabbed a thumb in the opposite direction, trying to ignore the heat from his hand pressed to her side.

"Pretty sure it isn't." His light brown eyes sparked with mischief, though his expression was neutral. "Let's just say I'm familiar with the layout of the hotel."

Of course, he was *familiar* with the hotel. He'd probably been there with countless women.

"Then I'm sure you're right." Dee pulled out of his

hold, inexplicably vexed by the idea of staying in a hotel where Tripp had visited other women.

This isn't a date. This isn't a date. This isn't...

They made another left at the end of a shorter hall and there was the elevator—just as Tripp had said.

To his credit, he barely gloated as he pushed the call button. She appreciated that.

They took the elevator to the main floor and went to one of the resort's two restaurants. The Silver Saddle was an elegant yet relaxed eatery with modern decor. There were leather and chrome chairs and dark wood tables. Leather booths in another section. And leather and chrome stools lined the bar.

Dionna surveyed the casually elegant space with its dim lighting and use of candles to make it feel warm and intimate. They were greeted by a beautiful woman with shiny red hair and a smattering of freckles over the bridge of her nose. Her smile was as big as Texas, and Dionna couldn't help relaxing a bit as she returned the woman's smile.

The woman showed them to their table, and Tripp pulled out her chair. Dee reminded herself that it wasn't a romantic gesture—simply a polite one, expected of Southern gentlemen.

"You seem to like the place." Tripp's warm gaze filled her body with heat and made her skin tingle.

Dionna's hands trembled slightly. The table for two suddenly seemed incredibly small. She needed a little space. Dee picked up her menu, creating a temporary wall between them.

"The decor is very nice," she acknowledged as she

studied the appetizers on the menu. "But it's a restaurant, so... I'll hold judgment until I have my meal."

"Fair point." Tripp's chuckle vibrated through her chest, despite him being on the other side of the table.

Her stupid tummy fluttered, and her cheeks filled with warmth in response to the sound of his laugh, which she'd come to adore during their chats the past couple of months.

Not a date. Not a date.

"In the mood for anything in particular?" Tripp asked.

"Not really." She figured he was studying his own menu, so it'd be safe to lower hers. She was wrong. Those twinkling brown eyes met hers and his full sensual lips curved in a lopsided smile. "I...uh..." She cleared her throat, her cheeks blazing. "Is there something you'd recommend?"

The amusement in Tripp's eyes indicated that he recognized how nervous he made her.

He shifted his gaze to the menu. "If you like steak, they make a great T-bone. If you're in the mood for lighter fare, I'd recommend the prawns, the cod or one of their vegetarian dishes. But if you're feeling adventurous, and I hope you are—" he glanced up at her again with that sexy cockeyed smirk "—I'd say let's go for the paella. It's made with a combination of seafood and pork. Sounds like a lot, I know. And it takes about a half an hour for them to make it, but it's worth every minute. I promise." He winked.

And there was that fluttering again. This time accompanied by a warmth that made other places on her body tingle.

"Sure. The paella sounds good." She dropped her gaze from his, silently chastising herself for behaving like a besot tween when, in fact, she'd just turned thirty-five on her recent birthday. *Pull it together, girl.* She snapped her knees together and cleared her throat as she studied the appetizers again.

"Perfect." Tripp clapped his hands, and the sound startled her, bringing her attention back to his handsome face. "And since you said you were starving, I'm not gonna make you wait that long to eat. Let's order a few starters, huh? Fried calamari, Serrano ham croquettes and montaditos sound good?"

"Yes to the first two." Dee loved calamari and the ham croquettes sounded delicious. "What are montaditos?"

"Basically, little open-faced sandwiches made on the most amazing crusty bread with a variety of toppings. There are two of each kind, so you'll get to try them all."

"Sounds wonderful." She closed her menu and pushed it aside. "Add a glass of white wine and I'm in."

They placed their order with the server who promised to return with their drinks—a glass of cava wine for her and a pale ale for him.

"Our conversations have always been about Ari and Ex's wedding. So tonight, why don't you tell me a little about you?" Tripp leaned back in his seat and sipped his water.

"You want to know about *me*?" Dionna could sense

the furrowing of her brows and made a point to relax them. She tucked a few of the loose twists behind her ear.

Tripp gazed at her expectantly.

"I grew up around the movie business. My father is a cinematographer and my mother is a set designer. I spent most of my career doing a variety of behind-the-scenes Hollywood jobs, which didn't make my parents very happy."

"Why not?" Tripp thanked the server who'd delivered their drinks.

"My father wanted me to become a lawyer. My mother hoped I would become a doctor. Neither of them wanted me to follow their career paths. Long hours, low-paid and nonpaying internships or apprenticeships in the business, which is pretty much exactly what I did." She laughed bitterly, but he didn't.

Instead, there was empathy in his eyes. This time, she felt the tiniest fluttering in her chest.

"I figured out pretty quickly that casting was what interested me most. So I interned and apprenticed for a variety of casting directors. Eventually, I got a job as an associate casting director for a tiny independent studio where I learned an awful lot but got paid very little. The rest you know." She shrugged, then sipped her glass of cava. "Ari hired me as a casting director when she started her own production company a couple years ago. End of story."

"And how long have you and Ari been friends?"

"More than twenty years." Dee smiled as she thought

about that first meeting with her best friend. "Which makes me feel ancient."

They met in the bathroom of their middle school. Ari had knocked on the panel between them and whispered loudly, asking if Dee had a tampon she could borrow. Dee had slipped one beneath the stall. As they washed their hands at the sinks, Dee noticed a bright red stain on the back of Ari's white capris. She offered Ari her sweater to tie around her waist. But she wasn't about to reveal any of that to Tripp.

"That secretive smile tells me there's more to this." Tripp shook a finger. "So come on. Let's hear it."

Dee was mortified. As if he could see the images inside her head. Knowing Ari, she would have no reservations about telling Tripp the full story. But it definitely wasn't the kind of dinner conversation she wanted to have with the man.

"We met in middle school. I was the awkward, quiet, shy new girl, and she was super popular. Of course. She borrowed a couple of things from me. One of which was a sweater that got ruined, so she wanted to replace it." Dee shrugged. "First, I'm pretty sure I became her project. She was determined to make me over as one of the popular girls. Along the way, we became good friends and both realized I shouldn't have to become someone else to fit in. I should just be myself. When her popular girlfriends wouldn't accept that, she ditched them. We've been best friends ever since."

"I'm glad you came to that conclusion." Tripp sipped his beer. "The people who truly matter accept us for who we are. Anyone who can't… In my experience, you're usually better off without them."

"Agreed." Dee nodded, her ex coming to mind.

"By the way, you look *incredible* tonight." Tripp set his beer on the table and gave her the kind of smile that probably made women melt.

"Thanks. But remember when I said Ari sent me a surprise package? This dress was one of the things she sent. The clothing is mine," she added. "I just hadn't packed any of it. Ari insists I should loosen up and enjoy this trip. That means not wearing my typical business attire."

"Sounds like Ari is a devoted friend. I have no doubt she'll be just as supportive and loyal a partner to my cousin." Tripp held up his nearly empty beer bottle. "To Ariana and Xavier."

Dee clinked her glass against the bottle. "To Ariana and Xavier," she echoed.

As she sipped her wine, she couldn't help thinking that Tripp Noble was nothing like she'd expected him to be.

Tripp watched as Dee took her first bite of the warm crusty bread piled high with melted blue cheese, unspeakably good homemade tomato marmalade and microgreens.

"My God, that's good," Dee muttered around a bite of the montadito. "Where have you been all my life? I meant the montadito," she said abruptly, one hand covering her mouth when her eyes met his amused ones.

He reined in a smile, not wanting to embarrass her

any more than she already seemed to be by the spontaneous statement.

"I'm glad you like it." He picked up the same variety she'd tried. It was one of his favorite variations. "Which one should we try next?"

Dee's dark brown eyes lit up. One corner of her mouth curved in a smile. He couldn't help wondering how those lips tasted and if she'd make the same soft moan if he kissed her good-night when he walked her back to her room.

Tripp shook the idea from his head.

Dee was adorable. Beautiful, without even trying. Glamorous when she did. Her all-business demeanor was nothing like the women he normally dated. Yet, something about her appealed to him. Tripp couldn't quite put a finger on what exactly it was about Dionna that he found fascinating.

"This one." She pointed to the montaditos piled with Manchego cheese, cured ham and sautéed spinach, onions and peppers.

"Let's do it."

They each grabbed one and took a bite. This time, he was pretty sure she purred. He felt the sound vibrating low in his gut and needed to shift in his seat.

"So far I'm impressed with the wine and the food," Dionna admitted. She spooned some of the fried calamari and a little of the accompanying sauce onto her small plate along with one of the ham croquettes.

"You almost sound disappointed." He added calamari and a croquette to his own small plate. "I told you Royal has some phenomenal eateries. Now do you believe me?"

"Total honesty?" Dee looked up from her plate, her brows furrowing.

"Please." He dipped a piece of the fried calamari into the sauce and popped it into his mouth.

Dionna's eyes studied his mouth for a moment. She sank her teeth into her lower lip and set her fork down. "I respect why Ariana changed the venue of her wedding. But I'm still a little resentful that you *guilted* her into moving it here to appease your aunt and uncle."

So he hadn't just imagined that Dionna had become snarkier in the video chats that followed Ariana's decision to change the wedding venue.

"Okay," he said simply.

His non-response seemed to irritate Dee even more. Her mouth tightened in an angry line as she poked an accusatory finger in his direction. "Do you have any idea how excited she was to have scored that cliffside castle for her wedding?"

"I can only imagine, and to be honest, I feel badly about that." Tripp finished his croquette and wiped his hands on a napkin. "I wanted to give Ariana a heads-up about how Ex's parents felt about a Hollywood wedding. I never expected her to move the wedding here. Still, I'd be lying if I said I wasn't glad she did."

Dionna's nostrils flared slightly. "I understand that Xavier has a deep connection to this place. That it'll always be his hometown. But Ari has a family, too. And her family and friends are in LA."

"Which is where they're going to be living," Tripp noted. He signaled the server for another beer. "They'll get to see the people in LA all the time. Only seems fair that the wedding is here, with the folks who knew him first, since we don't get to see him often."

"This isn't just about Ari's friends and family," Dee said. "Xavier's life is in LA, too. He also has friends there."

"And in Chicago and in New York," Tripp said. "I understand all of that. But what *you* don't seem to understand is that while Ex might be gallivanting all over the globe now, his *roots*—" he pressed his hands to the table for emphasis "—are right here in Royal. This will *always* be home for him. And he means a lot to the people here who've been cheering him on every step of the way. The entire town is excited about this wedding... Not just Ex's family."

Dionna frowned as she nibbled on her calamari. But she was beginning to see his side of this; he was sure of it. She just needed a little more convincing.

"Ari might've agreed to a change of venue. But she still wants the big, beautiful, show-stopping wedding she's always dreamed of." Dee leaned across the table and lowered her voice. "Yes, this resort and restaurant are impressive. But I'm still not convinced your little town—cute though it may be—is capable of putting on an event of that caliber."

Tripp's hands balled into fists beneath the table. He was trying to be reasonable about this. But Royal was as much a part of his blood as Ex was, so Dee's remark stung.

No one got to talk shit about his family. Not even Ms. Thick-Hips-with-the-Pouty-Lips across the table.

"This *little town* is home to a crap ton of millionaires, quite a few billionaires, high-profile business owners and CEOs, and an entire town of hardworking folks who care about Ex and about each other. And for the record, it's not like we haven't hosted important events that were plenty grand before." Tripp gritted out the words.

He didn't normally get worked up about things like this, but Dee's insults of the town felt like an acid-dipped dagger to his heart.

"I'm sorry if I offended you, Tripp. That wasn't my intention." Dee wiped her hands on a napkin and dropped them to her lap. "I know that what's best for Ex is your priority, but mine is what's best for Ari. I believe that subconsciously her reason for sending me on this mission solo is because she needs my honest opinion about whether having the wedding here is viable. She's far too in love with Ex to be objective about it, so I have to be. I'm sorry if that upsets you." Her tone and expression had softened.

Tripp wanted to remind Dee she *wasn't* doing this solo. He was just as invested in ensuring the success of this wedding. After all, they'd moved it to Royal because of him .

"Look, you have my word that I…and everyone in this town…are going to do our damnedest to ensure this wedding is the stuff of Ariana Ramos's dreams.

Trust me. Whatever it is that Ari wants, we can make it happen."

"Got any cliffside castles here?" Dionna stabbed another piece of calamari.

Tripp wanted to kiss that self-satisfied smirk right off of Dee's face. He sucked in a deep breath and picked up his fork, too. "All I ask is that you keep an open mind about having the wedding here in Royal."

"For Ari's sake, I will. Of course."

They finished their appetizers, mostly in silence. Then their server delivered the steaming, fragrant paella pan and set it in the center of the table. The arrangement of the lobster tails, littleneck clams, jumbo shrimp and chorizo made for a beautiful presentation, placed atop the golden Spanish bomba rice with pops of green and red from sautéed onions, peppers, fire-roasted tomatoes and a sprinkling of parsley.

"My God." Dionna pressed a hand to her chest and Tripp's gaze followed. Her brown skin gleamed and shimmered in the light. "What a stunning presentation."

"Wait until you taste it." Tripp spooned some of the steaming paella onto each of their plates, practically inhaling the savory scent of saffron, chorizo and sofrito. He waited for her to take her first bite.

Dee dug carefully into the paella with her wooden spoon, being sure to get a little of the lobster and shrimp. He watched as she spooned it into her mouth and chewed.

"Mmm…" The sound of Dee's murmur vibrated low in his gut. "Tripp, this is fantastic. This might be my new favorite meal. I could eat it every single day for the rest of my life and never tire of it."

"Told you it was worth the wait." Tripp finally dug into his own plate. "The paella is my favorite, but everything on the menu is delicious. There's something for everyone, including vegan and gluten-free options."

"You sound like an advertisement," Dee said. "You own stock in this place?" She shoveled more of the paella into that pretty little smart-ass mouth of hers.

"I wish. But I am trying to sell you on the place. I think it would be a great place to hold the bachelor/bachelorette party." Tripp studied her reaction.

Dee chewed thoughtfully as she glanced around, surveying the place with new eyes. "It is a really attractive space. And I know that Ari and Ex both want the prewedding party to feel more intimate than the ceremony and reception will be. The location—at the hotel where most of the guests will be staying— also seems ideal."

She was making his case for him, so he didn't feel the need to interfere. He just nodded and continued eating.

"But as ideal as the place seems, it feels pretty lazy to pick the first place we've seen." Dee took another bite.

"It's the first place *you've* seen," he noted. "I know every spot in town from fine dining to the super casual diner and the occasional food truck."

"You eat out a lot then." She glanced at him momentarily before returning her attention to her meal.

"When I'm not bumming a meal off my sister and her husband," Tripp chuckled. "They live on the ranch next door and their cook is pretty incredible. Helene could easily start a restaurant of her own."

Dee looked at him with renewed interest. "Let's put The Silver Saddle at the top of the list. If we don't find a more suitable option, I'm all for recommending that we have the prewedding party here."

A small victory. He'd take it.

"Now. It's your turn. Tell me more about you. You said your sister and her husband live next door. Do you have other siblings?" Dee took a sip of her cava.

"No, it's just me and Tessa. Xavier and his family lived on a connected property when we were growing up. He and I were more like brothers. I was also close to my neighbor Ryan Bateman, who is now my brother-in-law. So our family felt bigger than it actually was."

"And what was it like growing up on a ranch?" Dee peered at him intently as she ate her paella.

"It's hard work but also a lot of fun." Tripp smiled, thinking of all the happy times he'd had growing up on the ranch with Tessa, Ryan and Xavier. "I have so many great memories of the four of us hanging out together. Riding horses, feeding and caring for the animals, bale jumping, riding tractors, you name it. Though to be honest, even back then, ranch life wasn't really Ex's thing. Pretty early on, he knew he wanted a life away from the ranch."

He missed those days when their lives were simpler. And he missed spending time with his cousin, whom he'd seen very little of the past several years. Xavier was always on a deadline or off on a globe-trotting adventure.

Tripp's parents had moved out of the main house and now lived in a small homestead on the property, which they considered their retirement villa. A not-so-subtle hint that they were ready to begin traveling full-time, leaving the responsibilities of the ranch to him and Tess. In fact, his mother, father, aunt and uncle were currently on a three-week-long vacation in Cuba.

And now that Tess and Ryan were married, she helped him over at Bateman Ranch, in addition to her administrative duties at The Noble Spur. So the bulk of the responsibility of running the family ranch now fell to him.

"Sounds like a really nice way to grow up." Dee's soft smile made her dark eyes—the color of maple syrup—twinkle. He'd momentarily forgotten what she'd said. He was too captivated by her warm gaze and the way the candle flickering on the table reflected in her eyes.

"It was," he said finally. "But I'm surprised to hear you say that, Ms. Hollywood."

"You don't know everything there is to know about me, Tripp Noble." Her playful smirk elicited laughter from him. "I was born in LA, true enough. But my parents were originally from North Carolina. My paternal grandparents had a dairy farm where I spent most summers. I loved spending time there."

"Really?"

"*Yes!* Why does that seem so impossible to you? I'm not high-maintenance like Ari and Sasha." Dee plucked a clam from the shell and popped it in her mouth.

"Sorry if I can't imagine you frolicking in the hay and milking cows," Tripp chuckled.

"Well, I *did*!" Dee insisted, her words accompanied by a laugh. "My grandparents had four dozen cows. They didn't have any of that fancy automated machinery you probably use. So I got damn good at milking them by hand," Dee said proudly. "Ari and Sasha could never understand why I preferred to spend my summers on a farm with my grandparents and their dog."

"Why did you?"

"My parents worked long hours in the movie industry, and I was a latchkey kid. We couldn't afford the pricey summer camps that Ari and Sasha went to, so if I stayed in LA for the summer, it meant spending a lot of time alone. But I had the best time with my grandparents on their farm." Her eyes lit up.

"I'd imagine your grandparents worked long days on the farm, too," he said.

"They did. But I got to work right alongside them. They were loving and attentive. Doting, yet firm. They'd tell the most entertaining stories about life on the farm. I adored them and the slower pace of life there. It was a welcome change from the pressures of life in LA." There was a hint of sadness behind her smile.

"What's your favorite memory from your summers on the farm?" Tripp asked.

Dionna's smile widened, and she set her spoon down on the edge of her plate. "My grandparents had the sweetest dog—a golden retriever mix named Doug. After I got done with my chores every day, I'd pack my backpack with a few snacks and a notebook. Then I'd take Doug and we'd go on little escapades, exploring the area. I'd sit and write my own adventures. Then we'd head back home before it got too dark."

"So you're a writer?" Tripp set his spoon down.

"No. I haven't written anything since college. Even then, I never considered writing as a career. It was just something I did for fun. To let off a little steam." Dee suddenly looked bashful. She resumed eating.

"Seems like it gave you a lot of joy." Tripp shoveled a little of the rice into his mouth. "What kind of stories did you write? Romance? Mystery?"

The grin returned to her face and her eyes lit up again. "Epic fantasy. You know, high-stakes heroic adventures set in magical worlds. But the heroes were diverse. Not just the side characters playing the Minotaurs and dragons, hidden beneath layers of makeup and prosthetics."

"That sounds amazing," Tripp said. "I'd definitely read that. You ever think about trying your hand at writing again?"

"No. Like I said, it was just something I did for fun." Dee shrugged. He couldn't tell whether she was lying to him or if she believed it herself. "Besides, there are authors like N. K. Jemisin and Tracy Deonn already doing that."

"Thanks for the recs," he said. "But that doesn't mean there isn't room for more."

"I'm perfectly content with my career choice." Dionna frowned. Tripp had evidently struck a nerve. "Besides, my life is busy enough. Speaking of which, we only have a few days to work together on this wedding, and we have a lot to do."

"You're right." Tripp nodded. "Once we're done with dinner, I'll show you the other restaurant onsite. See if you think Ari would prefer that option."

"Great." Dionna seemed relieved he'd dropped the subject.

At the end of the night, he'd insisted on paying for dinner. After several rounds of debate, Dee finally agreed, then thanked him.

Tripp showed her The Glass House, the other restaurant at The Bellamy. But she agreed it felt too formal and that The Silver Saddle would be better.

At the end of the night, he walked Dionna back to her room—though she'd insisted it wasn't necessary. But there was no way he was going to let anything happen to the maid of honor at his cousin's upcoming wedding on his watch.

"Thanks again, Tripp. I thoroughly enjoyed the meal." She turned to him once they'd arrived at her hotel room.

"And the company?" he teased.

The reluctant smile that spread across her face reminded Tripp how beautiful Dionna was.

"The company was great, too. I had a really good time."

"Me, too," he said. "I'll be here bright and early to take you to breakfast."

"You don't need to walk all the way up here. I can meet you in the lobby," Dionna said.

"You evidently haven't met my parents," Tripp said. "I'm thirty-four and they'd still probably ground me if they knew I hadn't walked my...dinner companion to her door. I'll meet you here in the morning."

She narrowed her gaze at him when he'd nearly called her his date. Not intentionally, of course. But if he was being honest, the awkwardness of the night had definitely given him first date vibes.

"We're scheduled to meet the wedding planner at nine," Tripp said.

"At the Texas Cattleman's Club." There was a hint of distaste in Dee's voice. As if the venue couldn't possibly be suitable for her best friend's glamorous wedding.

He chose to ignore it.

"So how about I pick you up at eight thirty?"

"I'll be ready." Dee unlocked the door.

"Perfect," Tripp said. "Oh, and Dee?"

"Yes?"

"It was nice getting to know you a little tonight."

"You too, Tripp." Dee's face lit up. She went inside, closing the door behind her.

Tripp felt the slightest bit of tension in his gut. Dee still wasn't convinced they could make her best friend's dream wedding happen here in Royal. But he had no doubt of it.

He needed to focus on how he'd prove that to Dionna and stop imagining how it would've felt to kiss her good-night.

Four

Dionna sat at a table at the Texas Cattleman's Club with Tripp and Rylee Meadows—the wedding planner Ariana had hired. The woman was stunning with sparkling blue eyes, shoulder-length blond hair and a curvy frame.

Rylee had met them at the Texas Cattleman's Club that morning. She greeted them with a warm smile. Yet, there was tension behind it. She was clearly just as shaken as Dionna by the sudden change of venue from Los Angeles—her home turf—to Royal, Texas. But she hid her disappointment well.

Dee only recognized it because it matched her own feelings about the change. Still, they'd both been pleasantly surprised that the outer building and its interior space were much more glamorous than the club's name had led them to expect. According to Tripp, the club had been renovated and modernized a few times over the years.

"Breakfast was wonderful, Tripp. Thank you." Rylee dabbed her mouth with a napkin. "But it's time we get down to business."

Rylee stood, collecting her portfolio filled with notes, inspiration photos, drawings, fabric samples and other items. "Can we see the space for the wedding now?" she asked Tripp.

"Absolutely." Tripp ate the last bite of his breakfast croissant, wiped his hands on his napkin and stood. He extended a hand to Dionna, who was still seated.

Dionna really didn't need any help getting out of her seat. But Tripp had been something of a surprise. Yes, he was full of confidence and swagger. But he was also thoughtful and kind.

Dee had expected Tripp to go on and on about himself at dinner. Maybe brag about his family's holdings and estate in Royal. But he hadn't. And she couldn't help admiring how vehemently he'd defended his little town and the people here. There was more to Austin Charles Noble the third than she'd anticipated, and she'd enjoyed her time with him last night.

Dionna gave Tripp her hand. Her palm tingled and sparks danced up her arm as he helped her from her seat. Dee pulled her hand from his, startled by the unexpected sensation.

"Thank you." Dee forced a smile to counter his look of concern. She gestured ahead of them. "Lead the way. We can't wait to see the space we're working with."

"I've seen photos online," Rylee said as they followed Tripp. "But photos don't always tell the complete story. The aesthetics don't come to me until I get a chance to stand in the space with the couple's inspiration photos and samples on hand."

"That makes sense." Dee nodded. She found it similar with casting. Sometimes an actor who seemed like they would be perfect for a part just wasn't a good fit once she got to meet and audition them in person. "But your portfolio is amazing. I can't wait to see what you come up with."

Dee put a hand on Rylee's arm, slowing her down as Tripp got farther ahead of them. She lowered her voice. "If you honestly don't believe this space can rise to Ariana's expectations, I need you to be completely honest with me about that."

"If that's the case, I will." Rylee offered Dee a reassuring smile. "But if this is where Xavier and Ariana want to get married, I *will* turn it into the glitzy wonderland she envisions for her wedding. I learned quite a few tricks about how to transform just about any space into whatever my client wants it to be whether that's formal elegance, rustic charm, bohemian, whimsical or gothic." Rylee grinned. "Or vintage Hollywood glamour, which is what Ariana and Xavier have asked for."

"Which would've been much easier to produce if we were actually *in* Hollywood," Dionna muttered beneath her breath.

"True," the other woman acknowledged. "But don't worry, Dee. I'm up to the challenge."

"So what do you think?" Tripp turned to them. "This is the space Ex and I were thinking would work best for the reception. When you're done here, I'll take you to the outdoor space that would be a good option for the ceremony."

"I think this will do quite nicely." Rylee's blue eyes sparkled as she glanced around. "I see endless potential here. Give me a few minutes. I need to take photos and measurements."

"Take all the time you need," Tripp told Rylee. Then he approached Dee with a broad smile. "Not the dilapidated barn you expected, huh?" He nudged her with his elbow.

"No," she admitted begrudgingly. "It isn't."

Tripp was two for two, and he seemed pretty pleased with himself about it.

"Maybe I'm not so bad at this after all." His smug half grin was both sexy and maddening. The man certainly didn't lack confidence. Yet, he still managed to come off as genuine and chivalrous. Maybe it was a cowboy kind of thing.

Part of her wanted to elbow him in the gut. Part of her wanted to kiss him. Neither seemed advisable.

"Don't get cocky, cowboy. There's still an awful lot of wedding planning to be done. A viable space is a good start, but if the related services can't be sourced locally…" She shrugged. "Having the wedding here might not make sense. So I'd hold off on the self-congratulatory celebration for now."

"You're a tough cookie, Dee. But I happen to love a good challenge."

"Just remember this little 'challenge' of yours is the most important day of my best friend's and your cousin's life." She folded her arms and narrowed her gaze.

Tripp winked. "Yes, ma'am."

The man would probably be flirting with and trying to charm the panties off his home health aide when he was one hundred and lying on his deathbed. Seriously. Weaponizing that natural charm and charisma of his came as naturally to the man as breathing.

Never trust a shitload of charm and a smile.

"Look, I know we're still getting to know each other." Tripp was suddenly standing closer, his voice low. His subtle citrus and ginger scent wrapped itself around her like a warm hug. "And from the outside looking in, it might seem like I'm not taking this seriously. But I understand the gravity of the situation. I just feel life is too short not to enjoy every possible moment."

With Tripp in such close proximity, she could feel the warmth radiating from his brown skin.

Dee took a step back. Just far enough out of his orbit to regain her senses. Breathing came easier and so did rational thought.

"As long as you take this wedding seriously, I don't care if you wear a clown suit and flip cartwheels down Main Street. I only care that we complete our tasked mission before I board my plane home."

Tripp laughed so hard it drew the attention of Rylee who was measuring the windows and a few of the club staff who were preparing the room for an event.

Dee crossed her arms, planning to continue her stern stance with Tripp, but she couldn't help laughing, too. That had often been the case when they'd chatted. She'd be all business and superfocused, and he'd find a way to make her laugh.

She could understand Tripp's appeal. From a completely objective perspective, of course.

"Okay. Enough playtime, mister." She poked a finger in his side, nearly jamming her knuckle on his hard abs.

Never trust six-pack abs and a smile. Never trust six-pack abs and a smile.

"The space is nicer than I'd expected. But I'm not as confident as Rylee over there that we can transform it into the Old Hollywood glamour Ari is set on for her wedding." Dionna scanned the space again. "It's lovely. But it lacks the character and charm the LA property possesses. I realize Rylee is very good at what she does. But you can't make a silk purse out of a sow's ear." She borrowed a pet phrase of her late grandmother's, then added, "No offense."

"None taken." Tripp stepped behind her and placed his hands on her shoulders. He leaned down, his voice low. "Now, close your eyes."

"But…" She turned toward him, but the light pressure of his large hands pinned her in place.

"This will only take a minute, Dee. And it'll be worth it. I promise." His breath warmed her skin, his lips nearly brushing her ear.

Dionna's tummy fluttered and her thighs clenched. Electricity danced along her skin, emanating from where his hands rested. She squeezed her eyes shut, as he'd requested. "Okay."

Tripp stood up straight again, his hands still resting on her shoulders.

"Imagine this space decked out in vintage Hollywood glamour. We can do long tables with cream tablecloths and fancy vintage gold chairs. Tall gold vintage-style candelabra centerpieces. Arrangements of balloons in black, cream and gold. They can put down a black-and-white harlequin tile floor to really give the space that vintage look. Hang gold chandeliers. That'll lean into the Golden Age of Hollywood theme. String up some fairy lights to give it an ethereal feel. And I know a guy who has a stable of vintage cars. Most, he'll barely allow anyone to breathe on," Tripp chuckled. "But a few he rents out for special occasions. Having the bride arrive in a vintage car and the couple exit in it would really help set the scene."

Dionna stood there with her eyes shut, as Tripp had instructed. She'd been prepared to bat down his ideas. But she could see every element he'd described in her mind clearly. A hint of excitement stirred in her belly.

She hated to admit it, but Tripp was right. If they could pull off what he'd described, they could transform the Texas Cattleman's Club into the Old Hollywood glamour Ariana wanted for her wedding.

"You know Ariana best, so what do you think?" The weight of Tripp's hands was gone from her shoulders, and she immediately missed the warmth radiating from his body and the heat it ignited in hers. "Do you think she'd like it?"

Dee turned to Tripp in amazement. He'd come off as a jokester during their video chats about the wedding. But he'd clearly been paying close attention to what Ariana wanted for this wedding.

"Ari will love it. All of it." Dee's voice was softer and more sentimental than she'd intended. "And I have to admit I'm pretty impressed."

"As am I," Rylee said, a wide smile on her face. She clutched the portfolio in her hand. "I'd swear you've been reading my notes."

Rylee looked as impressed with Tripp's vision as she was. "I'd already planned to suggest a lot of what you just said, but I hadn't considered the harlequin floor." Rylee rubbed her chin as she studied the floor. "That would definitely take the Old Hollywood glam to the next level. So would the chandeliers." She glanced up.

Tripp could barely contain his grin.

"I usually work with a few LA- and New York-based vendors to rent these kinds of assets. But that would add substantial time and cost to the project, particularly given the time frame." Rylee shook a finger in Tripp's direction. "But according to Xavier, you're the person to talk to when it comes to sourcing items locally. So if you have local connections for any of this, like your friend who rents out the vintage cars, I'd appreciate it if you'd share those contacts and set up an introduction."

"You've got it," Tripp said.

He was so proud of himself Dionna was surprised

his puffed-up chest didn't pop the buttons off the denim shirt that highlighted his broad chest and the gun show he'd likely acquired from roping steer or whatever the hell ranchers did. The indigo shirt was a shade or two lighter than the dark washed jeans that hugged his impressive hindquarters.

Dee cringed inwardly.

Hindquarters? Pull it together, Dionna. He's a man, not a horse. And why are you looking at his behind anyway?

Never trust a guy with loads of charm, six-pack abs, a gun show, an impressive ass and a smile.

The list was getting hella long.

"Give me ten more minutes, then we can move to the outdoor space." Rylee was gone by the time Dee realized she was speaking to them.

Tripp regarded her with a lopsided grin.

Her nipples tightened and her belly fluttered. She squeezed her thighs together and cleared her throat, her face suddenly as hot as if she was standing in front of a furnace.

"What? I said I was impressed with your ideas." Dionna folded her arms over her chest, trying to remember if her bra was padded. "If you're expecting a cookie or applause—"

"The applause isn't necessary, but I will take that cookie. But only if it's homemade." Tripp unbuttoned his sleeves at the wrist and rolled them up, revealing a quick glimpse of tattoos on both his lower arms. "But what I'd prefer is that you have dinner with me tonight."

"Umm… Sure. Why not?" Her gaze lingered on the ink on his tawny-brown skin.

"Not the most enthusiastic acceptance of a dinner invitation I've ever had," Tripp chuckled. "But I'll take it."

"Sorry." Dee hadn't intended to stare, but she couldn't help trying to get a closer peek at Tripp's ink. "I didn't mean to sound…*not* enthusiastic. I was just a little preoccupied, I guess." She ran her fingers through her twists, worn loose again. Definitely not because Tripp had liked her hair down so much. But because, like Ari said, she was on vacation.

"You want a closer look?" Tripp asked.

"No." She shook her head, believing his response to be the adult version of "Take a picture already." It was a taunt often lobbed at her by the popular girls in high school when she'd stare at them with admiration.

"I don't mind." Tripp's gaze held hers as he extended both his arms so she could study the designs inked into his skin.

She should say no. Dionna realized that. But her hands and feet seemed to have a mind of their own. She stepped forward and reached out. "May I?"

"Of course."

Dee lightly traced the design etched into his brown skin. Cattle horns protruded from either side of a capital letter *N*. A line underneath the *N* ended in what looked like a spur.

She glanced up at him. "Is this your personal logo?"

"It's the cattle brand for our ranch, The Noble Spur."

Dee moved to the other arm, studying the tattoo.

It was a lovely illustration of a ranch surrounded by a split-rail fence. A bull grazed in the yard. A sign that read The Noble Spur hung from the archway over the entrance gate.

"So this is your family's ranch?" She glanced up at him again. Something in Tripp's intense gaze sent her stomach into somersaults. She swallowed hard and pulled her trembling hand from his arm. She stepped backward, nearly bumping into a passing employee.

"Careful!" Tripp pulled her to him, so she didn't crash into the server carrying a silver tray stacked high with glasses.

The near accident and being so close to Tripp, who felt and smelled amazing, made Dee's heart race and her hands shake.

"Thanks, Tripp."

"No problem." He released her. "And to answer your question… It isn't an exact spatial rendering of The Noble Spur. But it's a pretty solid representation of the house."

She studied his arm, fighting back the urge to trace his skin with her fingertips again. "It's stunning. The tattoo, I mean. I haven't seen the ranch."

Tripp's smile widened. "Consider this an open invitation. Come by anytime."

"Maybe next time." Dionna cleared her throat. "When I have more time and we don't have a wedding to plan."

"It's a date." Tripp's eyes danced with amusement when hers widened at his use of the word *date*. He'd probably used the word intentionally.

Dionna wouldn't give him the satisfaction of thinking he knew her that well. She swallowed her objection.

"Oh God! No, no, no."

Dionna and Tripp hurried toward Rylee Meadows whose hand was pressed to her open mouth as she stared at her phone.

"Rylee, what's wrong? Is there a problem with the venue?" Dionna asked.

"I wish it was something that simple." Rylee's skin blanched and her voice creaked. "That I could handle."

"So what is it?" Tripp asked.

"Are either of you familiar with Patrick 'Trick' MacArthur?" Rylee's voice was calm, but there was noticeable tension in her jaw when she uttered the man's name.

Tripp and Dionna shook their heads.

"Trick MacArthur is a juvenile, fame-seeking prankster who crashes high-profile weddings like this one. He makes his way into exclusive weddings and films himself pulling idiotic stunts for his audience of immature social media followers who find his brand of childish pranks hilarious." Rylee's distaste for the man seethed out of every pore, despite her placid tone.

"Okay, so the guy's an asshole," Tripp acknowledged. "From your reaction, I'm guessing you're concerned that he has his sights set on Ex and Ari's wedding. Why? Isn't there some bigger star remarrying his third or fourth wife for the second time?"

If the situation weren't so dire, Dee would've laughed.

"I deal with a lot of people in this business. And none of us wants his brand of publicity overshadowing our hard work," Rylee said. "I'm friendly with a server who works at a trendy restaurant in LA. Trick was there last night. The guy overheard him on the phone talking about Ariana and Xavier and saying that he'd learned through an exclusive source that the wedding was being moved to the groom's hometown of Royal, Texas."

"So he knows about Ari changing the location of the wedding. That doesn't mean that he plans to crash it." Dee hoped more than believed it to be true.

Rylee looked at her pointedly. "The last thing my source heard Trick say was, 'I've always wanted to go to Texas.'"

"Shit." Dee and Tripp uttered the word simultaneously.

"Do you have any idea how much Ari will freak out if some random upstages her at her own wedding?" Dionna was having heart palpitations just thinking about it.

"Trust me, I do." Rylee dragged a hand through her shoulder-length blond hair, and a puff of air escaped her cherry-red lips. "Having something like this happen at one of my weddings isn't a good look for me either."

"So what do we do?" Dee asked.

"I know what I plan to do if I catch his ass sniffing around this wedding." For the first time, Tripp looked genuinely distressed. "It's because of me they moved this wedding to Royal, and I promised Ari everything would be fine. I'm not going to let this guy ruin my cousin's wedding. Even if it means catching a case." Tripp struck his open palm with his fist.

"Calm down, cowboy." Dionna placed a hand on his tense arm. "The best man, who also happens to be the first cousin of the groom, getting arrested for assault isn't a good look either. Rylee is the expert here. I'm sure she'll come up with a more levelheaded solution."

"Like hiring a hit man," Rylee muttered under her breath, but they both heard her.

"Rylee! That's not helping," Dee said.

"I was joking. *Mostly.*" Rylee fluffed her bangs and sighed heavily. "Of course, I'll come up with a solution. One that doesn't involve bloodshed or anyone catching a case." The woman pointed a finger at Tripp whose chest expanded with each noisy breath. "I have no idea what that is just yet. But I promise you, I'll come up with something. So let's forget about Trick MacArthur for right now and focus on getting the plans for this wedding rolling. Tripp, if you're ready, I'd love to see the outdoor space you've been raving about."

Tripp didn't respond right away.

"Everything will be fine." Dee squeezed his arm. "And it's probably a good thing they moved the wedding here. It'll be easier to spot this guy and his entourage here in Royal than it would be in LA. This isn't your fault, Tripp. And I trust that Rylee will take care of it."

Tripp's eyes met hers. His expression softened, and the tension in his muscles eased. He nodded, his eyes filled with a mixture of gratitude and relief.

"The courtyard is through those doors." Tripp gestured toward a row of glass doors, and Rylee headed in that direction.

Before Dee could follow her, Tripp grasped her arm.

"Thank you for getting my head right on this." He kissed her cheek, then headed outside.

Dee stood there frozen. Her hand went involuntarily to the spot where Tripp's warm lips had quickly grazed her skin.

She sucked in a deep breath, then followed them out into the sunlight.

"Don't you dare fall for that cocky cowboy, Dionna Reed," she muttered to herself. But deep down, she knew that a tiny piece of her heart was already in a free fall.

Five

It'd already been a long day when Tripp parked at the restaurant.

He, Dionna and Rylee had spent a few hours at the Texas Cattleman's Club, where they also had lunch. Then they'd gone to visit florist Corryna Lawson at her shop, Royal Blooms. It had been Corryna's clever idea to create welcome bouquets for Dionna and Rylee. The women might've had reservations about entrusting a small local flower shop with the demands required by Ari and Ex's wedding spectacular. But such a personal preview of Corryna's work had undoubtedly swayed them.

And maybe he'd tipped Corryna's hand a bit by informing her of exactly what the bride envisioned for her wedding. So the sample options she'd created for them had blown Dionna and Rylee away. They were both on board and believed that Corryna was the ideal candidate to handle the floral arrangements for Ari and Ex's wedding festivities. They took photos to show Ari.

The celebrity photographer Ariana had hoped to book was doing a photo shoot for *Vogue Italia* the week of their wedding. Her second choice was doing a shoot for *Cosmo*. So Tripp had arranged a meeting with Seth Grayson, who was a local photographer. Both Rylee and Dionna were impressed with Seth's portfolio, but hesitant to engage a photographer who wasn't a well-known name in the industry.

Reluctantly, they agreed to recommend Seth to Ariana. But Dionna had essentially threatened his life if anything went wrong with the photos. Tripp was pretty sure Dee was only half joking.

While Rylee decided to walk around to get to know Royal, Tripp had dropped Dionna off at her hotel early that afternoon because she had a virtual casting meeting. He'd used the time to handle a few issues at the ranch, have a quick meeting with his sister about a potential vendor while entertaining his young niece and nephew, and grab a shower before picking Dionna up for dinner.

Tripp glanced over at Dionna again. He'd been sneaking glimpses of Dee the entire ride. He couldn't help himself. His eyes apparently had a mind of their own.

Dionna looked stunning again tonight. She wore a wrap minidress with buttons at the waist instead of a sash. The bold print in shades of green, hot pink, and blue looked good against Dionna's dark brown skin. The neckline of the dress revealed a hint of her full breasts. The strappy platform heels were sexy, yet practical. In other words: very, very Dionna.

The heels made Dionna's legs seem to go on for miles. His wayward brain couldn't help imagining how it would feel to have those long brown legs wrapped around his back.

"Are we waiting for someone?" Dionna glanced around.

"No. I…" Tripp loosened his collar and cleared his throat. "I just wanted to say that you look *really* beautiful tonight."

Dionna's glossy pink lips curved in a soft smile and her eyes twinkled. "Thank you. You look handsome tonight, too." She indicated his wool navy blazer, matching pants and white button-down shirt.

"Thanks." Tripp smoothed down his shirt. "I wanted to thank you again for keeping a level head when we learned about this wedding-crasher guy. And for helping me do the same."

Dionna's smile deepened. "Guess we make a good team after all."

"Yeah, I guess we do." Tripp nodded, unable to tear his gaze away from her full, kissable lips.

Dude, do not *fuck this up for me.*

Xavier's voice echoed in his head. Tripp tried to shake the vivid vision of him leaning in and kissing Dionna that had commandeered his brain.

Dee was a fiercely loyal friend. She was funny—

mostly when she wasn't trying to be. And yes, she was beautiful. But she was also off-limits per the promise he'd made to Xavier. So he wouldn't be kissing Dionna Reed tonight or any other night.

"Tripp, are you okay?" Dee touched his wrist, and a spark of electricity danced along his skin, startling him. He withdrew his hand immediately.

Her eyes were filled with genuine concern as she studied his face.

"You must be exhausted after the day we had plus whatever you had to do at the ranch. Don't feel obligated to entertain me every night. I could've grabbed something at one of the restaurants at the hotel." Dionna's smile was warm, but he could see the disappointment in her eyes, hear it in her voice.

"It has been a long day," Tripp said. "But I'm fine. Just got a lot on my mind." He clapped his hands together. "I've been looking forward to tonight. I hope you're hungry because you're in for another treat."

Dionna's eyes lit up and her smile deepened. "I'm starving, actually."

"Perfect." Tripp jogged around to the passenger door and helped Dionna out of the truck. Her subtle wildflower scent tickled his nostrils, and his palm felt warm against hers.

Just two more days.

He could keep his mind together and his hands to himself for that long.

They entered the all-glass building and were seated in a more private area of the restaurant, which still offered a view of the open kitchen where the chef and his staff worked their magic.

"This is a beautiful restaurant." Dee studied the elegant furniture and contemporary lighting. "I wouldn't have expected anything like this here in Royal." She frowned immediately, her expression filled with apology. "I just meant that with the glass facade, contemporary furniture and open kitchen... It's more like something I'd expect to see in LA."

"Fair." Tripp nodded. "But that's one of the reasons I brought you here tonight. You've got a very stereotypical idea about what to expect from a small Texas town. We're proud of our rich history of being ranchers and farmers. But there's much more to the town than that."

Dionna furrowed her brows, as if trying to decide how to phrase her response.

"You're overthinking it," Tripp said.

"I'm overthinking what?"

"Whatever you're attempting to say. So c'mon." Tripp gestured. "Out with it."

Dee sat taller and pulled back her shoulders.

"When you say there's so much more to the town... I'm thinking you mean compared to what the town was once like. I appreciate that," she said, when he nodded in response. "But most of the wedding guests reside in LA, New York, Atlanta, Chicago. Vibrant cities with lots for people to do. So they might not find the town quite as exciting as a longtime resident would."

Tripp tried not to look or sound as offended as he

was. "You're right. We're not carbon copies of any of those places. Nor do we want to be. Royal is filled with people, places and experiences far different than anything those cities have to offer." He tapped the table with a finger for emphasis. "If you'd open your mind to seeing that…you'd realize it, too. So maybe stop acting as if we're asking the guests to slum it for the weekend."

"I never said…" Dee snapped her mouth shut when he glared at her. "Okay, I might've implied it," she admitted. "I'm not trying to hurt your feelings or insult Royal, Tripp. I'm here to ensure my friend gets the wedding of her dreams. She's trusting me to do this because she knows I'll be straightforward about my feelings…good or bad. So I'm gonna need you to put on your big-boy chaps and not be so precious about your beloved little town when all I'm doing is stating a fact."

"I'm not being *precious*." He totally was. "All I'm saying is that your uninformed *opinion* of Royal does not equate to facts." He leaned on the table, arms folded.

"Uninformed?" Dee practically spat the word.

Tripp enjoyed her reaction more than he should have. At least he had the decency not to laugh out loud. Though he had a good chuckle about it in his head.

"I do *not* make decisions based on uninformed opinions, Tripp Noble." Dee wagged a finger in his direction.

Tripp could only imagine how heated her cheeks

were beneath her deep brown skin and perfectly applied makeup.

"I pride myself on doing thorough research, gathering available evidence, and then—*and only then*—making solid, educated, fully informed decisions." Dee folded her arms. The motion pushed up her breasts, dragging his attention to the shimmering skin and the hint of plump flesh revealed by the neckline of her dress.

He squeezed his eyes shut for a millisecond, reminding himself not to go there.

"Maybe that's the way you typically approach a situation. But you certainly haven't given Royal that same courtesy."

Before Dee could respond, two servers rolled out a cart with covered dishes on multiple shelves.

Dionna leaned across the table and whispered, "Why are they bringing us food? We haven't even placed our orders?"

"That's the other reason I brought you here. We could certainly have the wedding reception catered at the TCC as Rylee suggested. But I wanted to offer another option. I've asked Chef Colin Reynolds, the head chef here at Sheen, to prepare a sampling of possible offerings for a reception menu. If you're still hungry after the tasting menu, I'll buy you anything you want."

"So you didn't invite me to dinner just for my sparkling conversation, then?" Dee cocked her head and hiked a perfectly arched eyebrow.

Tripp chuckled and Dee dissolved into laughter, too. It eased the tension that'd been building between them.

"Why don't we call a temporary truce while we work our way through the delicious menu Chef Colin prepared for us? You can go right back to launching grenades at me and my beloved hometown when we're done."

"I'm *not* 'launching grenades.' I'm just trying to get this right for Ari. She's more than just my best friend. She's family, and she has *always* been there for me. So I won't let her down." Dee's tone was more solemn. "But I don't want to fight either. I'd much rather enjoy this lovely meal." She indicated the plates laid out in front of them.

"I'd like that, too." Tripp grinned. He turned to the server. "What do we have here, Delilah?"

Tripp could feel the heat of Dee's stare searing the side of his face. He chose not to acknowledge it. Instead, he remained focused on Delilah. If Delilah noticed Dee's reaction, her effervescent smile gave no indication of it.

"We have six options for hors d'oeuvres—prosciutto with freshly shaved parmesan and caviar with a smear of wasabi, an heirloom tomato caprese stack, shrimp cocktail shooters, mini buckets of tempura vegetables with a savory vegan mayo, delicious pork pot stickers and spicy lamb meatballs. The samples of red, white and sparkling wines are labeled. If you have any questions, just give me a call."

"You know I will." Tripp flashed the woman a smile. "Thanks, Delilah."

"Bon appétit!" Delilah bowed, her hands pressed together, then walked away.

Tripp surveyed the hors d'oeuvres laid out on the table. He rubbed his hands together. "I'm ready to dig in. You?"

Dee's expression was just short of a frown. She picked up the two small plates and handed him one without response. Then she carefully scooped one of each type of hors d'oeuvre onto her plate, and he did the same.

Dee spooned the caviar and prosciutto mixture into her mouth, and he did likewise. It would make it easier to compare notes if they sampled the items in the same order.

"It's good," Tripp said, feeling the need to fill the silence. "But I'm not a huge fan of caviar."

"Neither is Ari." Dee pulled her phone from her bag and typed out a few notes. "She tolerates it more than likes it. Pass."

"Agreed. What should we try next?"

"The heirloom tomato caprese stack?" Dee reached for it when Tripp nodded his agreement. They both murmured with delight as they bit into it. "Definitely a winner." Dee typed out notes on her phone again.

They tried the white wines next.

"I like the sauvignon blanc," Dee said.

"I prefer the Pinot Grigio," Tripp said simultaneously.

"I'm keeping a running list of items to consult the bride and groom on when we chat tomorrow morning," she said. "I'll add this to it."

"We should take that call together," Tripp said. "Since you're here and we've been working on this together... It just makes sense, right?"

Dionna shrugged. "Sure. Why not?"

"Anyone ever tell you that you have a real gift for making a guy feel wanted?"

"Sorry. I thought you might be...otherwise occupied at that time of the morning."

"Our ranch hands handle the weekends for us unless there's some emergency." Tripp bit into a pot sticker.

"Actually, I figured you and Miss Hors D'Oeuvres over there would be tangled up somewhere together." Dee cringed, as if she hadn't meant to say the words aloud. She picked up a pot sticker. "Not that it's any of my business."

"What makes you think there's something going on with me and Lilah?" He genuinely wanted to know.

"Well, you just called her by a pet name," Dee said. "Then there was the way you said her name. *Delilah.*" She uttered the word in a deep breathy voice.

Tripp nearly choked on his pot sticker. "I did *not* sound like that."

"Whatever you say, boss." She pinned him with a self-satisfied smile. "Though it wasn't all on you. There was the way she looked at you when she said, 'If you need anything, I mean *anything* at all, just call me.' And then you were all, 'You know I will, sweetcakes.'" Dionna seemed to be enjoying herself imitating both his and Delilah's Texas accents and mannerisms.

Tripp broke into laughter and so did she. He ate the last of his pot sticker. "You know that isn't what either of us said, right?"

"I might've taken a tiny bit of artistic license." Dee giggled, finishing her pot sticker, too. "But I think I got the general gist of the conversation. You two are a thing."

Damn. Was she that good or was his incognito game slipping?

"We don't have a thing." Tripp leaned in and lowered his voice. "We *had* one. Went out a few times a really long time ago. Chef isn't crazy about the staff dating customers, so we kept it on the low." He shrugged. "Lilah and I might not exactly be friends, but we are friendly. I make it a policy to end things on a pleasant note."

"Then I guess no one has ever broken your heart." The pain in Dee's voice made him want to reach across the table and squeeze her hand.

Tripp interlocked his hands on the table instead. His jaw tensed. "Actually, I have had my heart broken. It was devastating. That's why I made the conscious decision to take a more casual approach to dating and being up-front about that from the outset."

"Hmm..." Dee rested her chin in her palm as she studied him. "So you're *that* guy."

Tripp gave her a puzzled look. "Okay, I'll bite. What do you mean by *that guy*?"

"You're the 'I've been hurt before' serial dater who absolves himself of all the broken hearts he's left in his wake." Dee nibbled on another pot sticker.

"I never lead anyone on." Tripp tapped the table with his index finger. "I'm always up-front about my intentions."

"I get it. You enter each relationship with a label slapped across your forehead that reads *Warning: Does not do serious relationships. Ever.* You figure that if they catch feelings for you… Well, that's their fault. Right?" She finished her pot sticker and wiped her hands on a napkin. "But we both know you're fully aware that your charm can be…*intoxicating* for the average woman. That pearly white smile and dynamic magnetism pretty much drown out that warning. So when you eventually walk away and leave her brokenhearted, you're all, 'Sorry, babe, but I tried to warn you I'm not a stick-around-forever kinda guy.'"

Tripp was irritated by her imitation of him this time. Mostly because it was a little too on-the-nose.

But he didn't need to justify his life choices with Ms. Dee "I-Know-Every-Damn-Thing" Reed. "No one I've dated thus far has complained. So maybe us Texans are a little more progressive than you think." He winked, determined to show her that he was unbothered by her armchair analysis of his romantic life.

"I honestly think you believe that. But if you had a candid conversation with those exes you're so friendly with, I wonder if they'd agree." Dee analyzed the plates in front of them. "Lamb meatballs?"

Tripp frowned, more irritated than angry. With himself more than Dee. Because for the first time, the slightest doubt crept into his mind about his dealings with his exes.

Were they really as okay with the ending of the relationship as they had seemed?

"Shrimp cocktail shooters," Tripp said gruffly, feeling the need to disagree with this woman who seemed dead set on killing his easygoing vibe.

Dee froze, her hand suspended above one of the meatballs. "Shrimp cocktail it is."

They both took a bite of the jumbo shrimp and tangy cocktail sauce.

"This is a winner," they said simultaneously, then laughed.

"If Ari was here, she'd say jinx." Dee smiled. She finished her other piece of shrimp, then typed out more notes. "Meatballs next?"

He nodded, plucked one of the lamb meatballs wrapped in a roasted sugar snap pea from his plate and took a bite. The savory meatball was juicy and delectable. Roasting brought out the sweetness in the pea.

"Delicious." Tripp discarded the toothpick and plucked the other meatball from his plate.

"They are really good." Dee shoved her plate toward him, indicating that he should take her other meatball.

"I thought you said you liked them?"

"I do. But we have a lot more food to try. I'm pacing myself," Dee said. "Plus…you know you want it," she teased.

He did. And he wasn't just thinking about that damn meatball.

The more this woman got under his skin, the more he wondered about the taste of her full lips.

He accepted the meatball and thanked her. Then they both tried the tempura vegetables and vegan mayo.

"I didn't think I'd like this." Tripp nibbled on the last veggie fry. "But these vegetable straws are really good. And that vegan mayo is the truth."

"Coming from a cattle rancher, that's high praise indeed." Dee typed out more notes. "And we definitely need vegan options."

"Five out of six are winners. Not bad, eh?" Tripp stacked their empty plates after Dee offered him the remainder of her fries. "I don't want to brag here..."

"You absolutely do," she countered with an eye roll.

"Maybe a little." He peered through his thumb and forefinger. "And since our local vendors have been blowing you away, I've been thinking... Why don't we make a point of choosing local vendors? It would be good PR for Ariana, Xavier, the town of Royal and the individual vendors. Plus, it would spread a lot of goodwill among the locals. Isn't that a huge part of the reason Ari moved the wedding here in the first place?"

"I don't know, Tripp," Dee said. "There's a bakery in LA that Ari has her heart set on. She has a makeup artist she works with regularly, and she's already engaged her stylist Keely Tucker, who is also a friend, to create her custom wedding dress. There's no way Ari will want to work with anyone else."

"The makeup artist and wedding dress designer... I get that. But transporting the cake from LA to Royal opens up the possibility of a slew of disasters. An unnecessary risk, given that we have a phenomenal bakery right here in town. I've seen them make some stunning wedding cakes. We could pop into the shop tomorrow. If I give her a call right now, I'm sure she could fit in a tasting for us tomorrow."

"Has anyone ever told you that you are incredibly persistent?"

"If that's code for pest…then yeah," Tripp chuckled. "Is that a yes?"

Dee heaved a quiet sigh, her eyes narrowing. "Fine. Yes."

Tripp made the call to his favorite local bakery, glad Dee was amenable to the idea of going almost exclusively with local vendors. But he honestly wasn't sure if the sense of satisfaction he felt was because he was slowly winning the battle or because it meant he'd get to spend more time with Dionna.

Six

There had been a few tumultuous moments during the evening. But they'd sketched out a possible menu and agreed to recommend that Sheen cater the wedding reception. Ari and Ex could always make changes, but Dionna felt good about the solid options they planned to present to the couple. By the end of the evening, she could finally breathe a sigh of relief.

There were still a few important items to address during their group chat with Ariana and Xavier the next day. Then on Sunday, she'd order a car service to the Dallas/Fort Worth International Airport and take a direct flight back home to LA.

When she'd first learned that her best friend wouldn't be coming, she'd been counting down the hours until she could escape this town and board that plane home.

But in spite of herself, she'd managed to enjoy her time here with Tripp. She'd gotten a kick out of needling him a bit. And it seemed that he had a knack for getting under her skin.

What she hadn't expected was just how palpable the attraction she felt to Tripp would be. It was like a living, breathing thing that seemed to take up space between them. She could feel it whenever those mesmerizing brown eyes of his flickered over her skin. Whenever he touched her wrist or pressed a hand to her back as he guided her through a restaurant or across the street.

Her skin felt as if it was on fire. Her nipples tightened. And there was the sweetest ache between her thighs.

She was much too old to have a rabid crush on the handsome cowboy who would probably be holding on to his international player's card until it was wedged out of his cold dead hands.

Not the kind of man she should be interested in. Besides, he lived in Texas and she lived in California. End of story.

Dee sighed. Why was she even thinking about this? The only thing going on between her and Tripp was the lustful thoughts happening inside her head.

"I forgot to ask what you're working on at the production company?" Tripp asked as they finished the evening with two espresso con panna.

"We're in the early stages of an ambitious project that's far different than anything we've done before.

It's a Western about a Black cowboy in Texas who has to fight to keep his land."

"Sounds like the story of my family," Tripp said, his expression suddenly serious. "When my great-grandfather first acquired the land in the early nineteen hundreds, folks who owned property around here did just about everything they could to make him give up the title to his land."

Dee's chest ached from the pained look in Tripp's eyes. He didn't want to talk about this, and who could blame him?

"Ariana mentioned that Xavier's family…your family had a similar experience, but she didn't go into any of the details." Dee set down her coffee cup.

"Acceptance was a long process for my great-grandparents and grandparents. I guess that's where I get my stubbornness and occasional ornery streak." He attempted a small smile.

"Well, that stubborn streak has served you well. Your ancestors would be proud of everything your family has achieved," Dee said sincerely. "But I'm sorry for bringing it up. I should've realized that the topic might be upsetting."

Tripp placed his hand on her wrist. His gaze was warm. "It didn't upset me. Yes, the topic hits close to home. But it's an important story. One people need to know about. People need to know about the existence of Black farmers and ranchers—*then and now*. Their history has been buried. So I'm excited to see more projects like this happening. Where do you plan to film the movie?"

"There are a number of studios around LA or in the desert that—"

"Wait… You're making this movie about a Black cowboy in Texas, but you plan on filming it in Cali?" Tripp's expression shifted. He released her hand and shook his head. "Not gonna lie. That fucking sucks."

"I know, but it's easy and efficient. Central to all the players." Dee sipped her espresso. "It's something that's done frequently in the industry."

Tripp looked sad.

"I feel like I accidentally told a wide-eyed little boy that Santa isn't real." Dee squeezed Tripp's wrist this time. Her tone was teasing, but she'd said the words with genuine empathy. "You look so disappointed right now."

"Good. Because I am. Damn green screen," he muttered the last words beneath his breath, and Dee couldn't help laughing.

"Sometimes it's just really amazing set design. Like the show *Friends*. It was set in New York but filmed on the Warner Brothers set in Burbank. *Casablanca* wasn't filmed in Morocco. It was filmed in Burbank, too. And *Scarface*—"

His eyes widened. "Don't tell me…"

"Most of the movie was filmed in California. Sorry." She shrugged, moving her half-finished espresso aside, already beginning to feel a little too wired. "But that's the magic of the movies. They can take us to outer space, to the future or to a city on the other side of the world and make it completely believable."

A soft smile curved one edge of Tripp's mouth,

making him look even more delicious than he already did in his navy blazer that clung tightly to his impressive biceps.

"What?" Dee asked. "I'm geeking out about this, right?"

That picture-perfect smile of Tripp's expanded. "That's not what I was thinking."

"What were you thinking?" Dee leaned forward, her arms folded on the table.

She was afraid she might not like his answer. Still, she couldn't stop herself from asking.

"Honestly? I was thinking about how beautiful you are. More so when your eyes light up like that and you're practically glowing from within because you're bursting with excitement." Tripp drank more of his espresso. "It's incredibly cute."

Incredibly cute? Like a puppy? Just what every woman wants to be called.

Then again, he'd also called her beautiful.

"Thank you." Dionna ignored the heat rising in her cheeks. "And I'm totally at ease with the fact that I can be an unabashed geek when it comes to what happens behind the scenes in the film industry. Casting, set design, costume design, mixing, editing, you name it. I was a goner the first time my parents took me on set when I was about eight. There's been no turning back ever since."

"It's great that you're in an industry that you're so passionate about." Tripp switched to drinking his water with lemon. "I envy that."

"You're not passionate about ranching?" Dee asked.

"Ranching is in my blood. The thing I was born to do." He gave a half shrug. "I enjoy life on the ranch, and I'm honored to continue my family's legacy."

"But?" Dee propped her chin on her fist and studied his face.

Tripp sucked in a deep breath. "Sometimes I do wonder what my life would've been if I hadn't been born into a role, you know?" He folded his hands on the table, mere inches from her fingertips.

Dee fought back the urge to reach out and squeeze his hand. "It's never too late to do something different with your life, if that's what you really want, Tripp."

"Xavier opted out of ranch life over a decade ago. My sister married the rancher next door four years ago, and she has two young children. That makes me the heir apparent by default. There's no way, after everything my grandparents and great-grandparents went through to hold on to this ranch, that I'd let it go to someone else. And if I don't carry on the family tradition, that's *exactly* what would happen."

There was a mingling of pride with a hint of sadness in his eyes. Her heart ached for him. Maybe he did enjoy being a rancher. But in some ways, it seemed he felt as if his life was not his own.

"That's a heavy burden to bear," Dee said.

"Maybe. But what I do matters. I have a good life. Wonderful family. Great friends. The freedom to expand my interests would've been nice," Tripp acknowledged. "But I'd never want to call any place but Royal home. I love it here."

"It must be an amazing feeling to be so rooted in

a place and to know without a doubt that's where you belong," Dee said.

"You live in LA and love being part of the film industry." Tripp looked puzzled. "I'd think that you'd be in heaven."

"I do love the industry and stepping behind the magic mirror of filmmaking. But I don't love the traffic and the hustle and bustle of life in LA." It pained her to say it, but it was true. LA living was the price she paid for doing work she loved.

"So if you could be in the film industry but live anywhere you wanted, where would that be?" Tripp leaned forward, his chin resting on his open palm.

Dionna smiled. "I'd live on a little farm like the one my grandparents owned."

"What happened to your grandparents' farm?"

Dee frowned, her heart breaking at the thought. She cleared her throat and sighed. "My grandparents were really proud people. So when Grandad got ill, he didn't want us to know how serious it was. Nor did he want us to know his treatments and hospitalizations were draining them financially. They got a second mortgage on the farm. Then they sold it. By the time we knew any of this, it was too late. They'd already sold the place for a cut-rate price and my grandfather only had a few months to live." She dragged a finger beneath her eyes, trying her best not to ruin her makeup.

Who knew I'd need waterproof mascara tonight?

"I'm sorry that happened to your grandparents, Dee." Tripp handed her the handkerchief in his pocket.

It was white with a navy, purple and black abstract design.

"I can't. My makeup will ruin it," she objected.

"It's okay." He shoved it in her direction again. "Plenty more where that came from."

Dee thanked him and accepted the hankie. She dabbed at the corners of her eyes.

"Remember when I said my parents didn't want me to follow them into the film industry? The last thing my gram said to me before she died was, 'It's your life, sweetie. Not your parents. Follow *your* dreams. They'll get over it.'"

"Did your parents get over it?" Tripp asked.

"They were furious. They said I was wasting my gifts in an industry that would never truly appreciate them." Dionna winced, recalling the conversation she'd had with her parents. "My dad didn't speak to me for a year. They weren't used to me going against them. I spent my entire childhood trying to be their perfect little girl. I know my parents love me. But sometimes it felt like being exactly who they wanted me to be was the only way I could get them to show me that they did. To say that they were…" The words caught in Dionna's throat and her eyes burned with tears.

"Proud of you?" Tripp squeezed her hand.

Dee nodded, dabbing beneath her eyes with the hankie.

Why had she allowed herself to get worked up about this again? It was ancient history. This had happened seventeen years ago. Still, her heart felt as raw as if it'd happened yesterday.

Dionna tugged her hand from Tripp's and forced a smile. "Sorry. I'm *really* tired. Is it okay if we call it a night?"

"Of course." Tripp stuffed several bills into the black leather folder, then shoved a copy of the bill in his shirt pocket. He stood, holding his hand out to her. "Shall we?"

Dee slipped her hand in his. They waved good-bye to Delilah and to Chef Colin who'd come to their table to introduce himself to Dee when the entrées had been brought out to the table. Then they walked to Tripp's truck in a silence that felt...comfortable.

On the way to the hotel, Tripp made small talk. Recapping some of their favorite foods and wines. Making her laugh by reminding her of some of the funny moments they'd shared over the course of the day. By the time he pulled his truck into the parking lot of The Bellamy, she didn't object to him walking her to her room. Because if she was being honest, she wasn't ready to say good night.

They got off the elevator on the third floor and made the trek to her room, still chatting about the films she knew of that had been filmed someplace other than where the story was set. Finally, they reached her door.

"Thank you, Tripp. I have to admit that this wedding planning experience has been a lot more fun than I expected. You've really come through with the vendors so far. Are you sure this isn't your side hustle?" Dee teased. "Because you're really good at it. Even when you're dealing with a tough customer."

"I've always enjoyed finding ways to connect the right people." He shoved his hands in his pockets. "If I could figure out how to make it a side hustle, I would." He grinned. "But I wouldn't call you a tough customer. You're a dedicated friend. One Ari is damn lucky to have." Tripp winked.

Dionna's tummy fluttered. A wave of warmth made its way down her spine, and her pulse raced. She waved her small bag, which contained her room key, in front of the lock and it clicked. Dee pushed the door open and stepped inside. She glanced at the refrigerator, where she had a bottle of wine chilling that she'd purchased earlier in the day.

Tripp seemed as reluctant as she was to say their goodbyes. The seconds of silence ticking by felt like minutes.

"Thank you again, Tripp. For everything." Dee dropped her bag on the table near the door. "Would you like to join me for a nightcap or maybe some really overpriced chocolate from the minibar?" She laughed nervously, the words rushing from her lips before she could stop herself.

What are you thinking?

She needed to create distance between herself and the ridiculously handsome cowboy she'd become far too fond of. Not scheming ways to spend more time with him.

Tripp opened his mouth, and Dee was sure he was going to say yes. But he dragged a hand down his handsome face and released a quiet sigh. His smile was polite, not the genuine one he'd flashed her moments earlier.

"I wish I could, Dionna. But like I said, it's been a really long day. I need to handle a few things early tomorrow before I meet you here for that chat with Ariana and Xavier at ten. I should call it a night."

Or you could just spend the night here.

For a moment, Dee wasn't sure whether she'd said the words aloud or if she'd only said them in her head. When Tripp didn't react, she breathed a sigh of relief.

"I thought the ranch hands handled weekends."

Why couldn't she keep her mouth shut?

Tripp was trying to turn her down politely, and she'd just made it awkward.

"Typically. But some things I prefer to handle myself."

They stood in silence for a few painfully awkward moments.

"Well, good night then," Dee said finally.

She moved to shut the door, but Tripp leaned and dropped a kiss on her cheek. His beard abraded her skin.

"Night, Dee," he said. When he stepped back, his eyes locked with hers for a moment before his hungry gaze dropped to her lips.

Suddenly, her skin felt as if it was on fire. And there was a steady pulse between her thighs.

"See you in the morning." Tripp turned and strode back toward the elevator.

Her heart thudding in her chest, Dee's hand went to the spot where Tripp's lips had touched her skin.

Maybe it was a good thing Tripp had turned down her invitation. Clearly, that irresistible charm of his was starting to work on her, too.

Seven

The next morning, Tripp stepped off the elevator and made his way to Dionna's hotel room. At this point, he was beginning to wear a path in the carpeting.

Tripp sighed, trying to cleanse his brain of the thoughts that had kept him awake staring at the ceiling until the wee hours of the morning.

Dionna Reed was living rent-free in his brain, and he wasn't even sure why. They were complete opposites. She was all buttoned-up and straitlaced with her to-do lists, research and endless note-taking. While he was more of a go-with-your-gut kind of guy.

And yes, they'd had a few laughs and managed to enjoy each other's company. But there had been more than a few moments when they'd rubbed each other the wrong way.

So why couldn't he stop thinking about her?

His brain had insisted on replaying Dionna's bright smile and contagious laugh. And her sweet, subtle spring scent seemed to linger in his senses long after he'd showered before bed.

The teasing lilt of Dee's voice had drowned out the urgency of Xavier's when he'd made Tripp promise not to get involved with her.

Every time he'd touched her—even in the smallest, most insignificant ways, like guiding her through the restaurant door—he'd gotten a little thrill. Like when he was a kid and would tread as close as possible to the lines his parents had told him not to cross.

He stood in front of her door at twenty to ten, took a deep breath and knocked.

Dee opened the door wearing a white terry cloth robe. She tightened the belt at her waist, then smoothed back her twists piled atop her head.

"Sorry, but you're early and I'm running late." She opened the door to let him in and gestured toward the sofa. "I went to the gym this morning and there was a wait for a treadmill. Time got away from me."

"It's my fault. Like you said, I'm early. I thought you might want to go over a few things before we chat with Ari and Ex." Tripp shoved his hands in his pockets and tried really hard not to think about whether or not Dee was naked beneath that robe.

The way she was clutching at the fabric shielding her chest with one hand and the fabric covering her thighs with the other, he was betting she was.

"Talking beforehand would've been a terrific idea…

had I known in advance." Dee hiked one eyebrow, and her nostrils flared.

"Should've suggested it last night. Sorry. Just pretend I'm not here." Tripp headed for the sofa. "This'll give me a chance to address the emails I didn't get to yesterday."

"I was about to step into the shower. In fact, I left it running." Dee nodded over her shoulder toward one of the two bedrooms in the suite. He could hear the faint sound of water running. "Have a seat. Help yourself to anything in the minifridge. And I ordered breakfast, so could you let them in if they come while I'm in the shower?"

"Sure thing." His eyes were drawn to the flashes of smooth brown skin revealed when she released the robe to rummage through her purse.

"Here." Dionna extended several bills.

"What's this for?" Tripp didn't reach for it.

"For the tip," Dionna said.

"Don't worry. I've got—"

"Ari paid for my room and travel, and you've paid for *everything else* since I arrived. I think I can afford to tip."

"I don't mind." Tripp dug his hands deeper in his pockets.

"Take the money, *Austin*." Dee shook the bills.

Shit. She'd gone government name on him again.

"Fine." Tripp raised his hands in surrender, then accepted the cash.

"Great." Dionna tossed the word over her shoulder as she hurried off, that damn robe swishing behind her.

Tripp tossed the bills on the table and sank onto the leather sofa. "Stubborn, recalcitrant woman," he muttered under his breath.

It was a phrase his grandfather and father often used about their better halves. The phrase was almost always accompanied by a head scratch and a reluctant chuckle or grin.

After thirty-four years of life, Tripp was beginning to understand.

How could Dee be so damn exasperating, yet also so incredibly appealing?

Maybe he was a masochist who enjoyed banging his head against a wall. Or maybe…

Tripp shook his head. Dionna Reed answering the door wearing nothing beneath her robe was the very last thing his overactive imagination needed.

One more day, then Dee is heading back to LA.

Tripp should've been relieved. Once Dee was gone, he could stop gallivanting around town playing the role of Royal's one-man convention and visitors bureau slash weekend wedding planner. Then he could return his focus to running the ranch. Only, the more time he spent with Dee, the less excited he was about her leaving.

Ten minutes later, Dee emerged from the bedroom in a cream off-shoulder sweater, slim black pants that highlighted her delicious curves and a pair of black riding boots. Half of her hair was pulled back by a fancy gold barrette. The loose twists dusted her shoulders. And for the first time since she'd arrived, Dee was wearing her glasses. These were dark brown accented by gold rhinestones and gold trim. Jimmy Choo was emblazoned along her temples.

On a one-to-ten scale of hot librarian vibes, Dee was dishing up a solid twenty.

"Dee." Tripp stood, unable to tear his gaze away from her. He rubbed the back of his neck where flames licked at his skin. "You look...*fantastic*. The glasses—"

"The pressure in the shower is a little *too* good." She shrugged. "I accidentally sprayed myself in the face and blasted one of my contacts down the drain."

Tripp tried his best not to laugh, but when Dionna did, he couldn't help joining in.

"Well, I'm sorry you nearly lost an eye while showering." Tripp almost managed to keep a straight face. "But I was going to say, I've never seen you in those glasses before, but they look really good on you."

Honestly, he couldn't imagine there was much that wouldn't look good on Dee. But the hot brainiac look she was serving up in spades was something he hadn't known he needed in his life.

"Thanks." Dee pushed her glasses up the bridge of her nose, her mouth curved in a bashful smile.

His heart pounded, the knocking sound in his chest echoing in his ears. Could Dee hear it, too?

"Tripp?" Dee waved a hand in front of his face. "Ari and Ex will be calling soon. I need to grab my planner and notebook. Could you get the door? That's probably room service." Dee gestured toward the door: the source of the *actual* knocking.

He wasn't sure if he should be relieved because the

knocking was real and not coming from his chest…
like some lovestruck animated character. Or if he
should be alarmed that he'd zoned out for a minute…
like a lovestruck animated character.

Either way, he needed to get it together. *Now.*

Dionna retrieved her planner and notebook, her
stomach still fluttering from Tripp's compliment.

Girl, you really *need to get out more.*

Her best friend's plea echoed in Dionna's head.
"Dee, don't take this the wrong way, sweetie, but you
need to get a life."

She had a life. A damned good one. A job she loved.
A few good friends. Her parents were still alive, which
she was grateful for, even if they drove her crazy. And
a tiny overpriced apartment in LA that she could actually afford.

What more could a woman want?

"Ready to eat?" Tripp's deep, sexy voice snapped
her out of her temporary daze.

That was what more this woman could want. A
man who was charming, funny, incredibly sexy and
who looked at her like she was his last meal.

Dee clutched the planner and notebook against
her chest to hide the swell of her nipples against her
Angora sweater. She swallowed hard, her throat dry
as she ambled over to the dining table where Tripp
had rolled the service cart bearing their breakfast.

"I wasn't sure what you'd want, so I ordered everything." Dionna lifted the silver domes to reveal bacon

and sausage, pancakes and waffles, scrambled eggs and eggs over easy, plus a variety of juices.

"Perfect." Tripp rubbed his hands together, his light brown eyes gleaming in the Saturday midmorning sun. "Ready to dig in?"

"First, I was thinking we should move our seats closer together, opposite the window." Dionna gestured toward the light streaming in and warming her face. At least, she assumed that was the reason her face suddenly felt so hot. "To get the best lighting for our call," she clarified when Tripp gave her an amused look.

"Yes, ma'am." Tripp shrugged, sliding his chair over, opposite the window she'd set up her iPad in front of.

"According to Ari, perfect lighting is the first rule of film. Especially for those of us with darker skin."

"Your skin always looks radiant in those video calls." Tripp reached for the metal handle of the glass syrup dispenser. "So I'll take your word for it. Syrup?"

Tripp held the dispenser aloft, and with the sunlight shining through the glass container, the liquid inside was nearly the same soft brown as Tripp's eyes.

"Please," she said.

Tripp poured syrup on her waffles until she'd indicated it was enough, then poured some on his pancakes. Since she was still standing there, her brain apparently short-circuiting with Tripp in such close proximity, he moved her chair beside his and gestured for her to have a seat.

She thanked him and did just that.

They ate in companionable silence except for the occasional commentary on how good the food was. And though this was now the fifth consecutive meal she'd eaten with Tripp, something about the two of them sitting so close together felt more...*intimate*.

A shiver rippled up Dionna's spine, and she dropped her fork. The metal clanged against her plate, bounced onto her pants, then onto the carpeted floor, splattering syrup along the way.

She moved to retrieve the wayward utensil, but Tripp squeezed her arm.

"I've got you." His luminous grin made her feel all kinds of awkward and apparently rendered her speechless.

Tripp retrieved the fork, carried it to the small bar sink, then opened the drawer that contained a full set of silverware. Dee tried not to think about why Tripp knew *exactly* where to find a fork in her hotel suite.

Let's just say I'm familiar with the layout of the hotel.

"Thank you." She flashed an awkward smile and accepted the new fork. "I'm not usually this clumsy, I swear." Dee shoved a fork full of the fluffy Belgian waffles in her mouth.

Tripp handed her a damp dishcloth so she could wipe the syrup off her pants while he stooped to clean the splash of syrup off the carpet using a soapy paper towel.

Dionna's blood seemed to heat to a simmer as Tripp kneeled on the floor beside her.

Imagine him kneeling like that, but in front of you.

Dionna cringed. Her best friend's dirty mind and wicked sense of humor had rubbed off on her more than she realized. She shook the thought from her head, muttered her thanks again, then wondered aloud why Ari's call was already ten minutes late.

"Sounds like things are pretty wild for both of them right now." Tripp discarded the paper towel, washed and dried his hands, then joined her at the table again. "I wouldn't be surprised if they needed to reschedule."

"I hope not," Dee muttered. "The longer it takes us to hammer out the details of this wedding—"

"The more time you'll be forced to spend with me?" There was a teasing lilt in Tripp's tone and a half-hearted smile. But there was disappointment or maybe hurt in his eyes.

Dionna felt like the Wicked Witch of LA.

"That isn't what I was going to say," Dee said truthfully. "And the past couple of days have actually been…"

"Surprisingly fun?" This time Tripp's smile felt more genuine.

An involuntary smile spread across Dionna's face. She nodded. "Yes. Exactly that."

"Good. Because I've enjoyed hanging out with you, too." Tripp nudged her shoulder playfully.

Heat filled his brown eyes. When his gaze dropped to her mouth, it felt as if she'd forgotten how to breathe. But this time she managed to hang on to her fork.

Her phone and iPad rang simultaneously. Dee sucked in a much-needed breath and accepted the call.

"We were beginning to think you two had forgotten about us. Don't y'all know people got shit to do around here." Tripp's wide smile and playful Texas twang belied the irritation conveyed by his words.

Ariana and Xavier laughed, both of them looking and sounding guilty.

"Sorry, you two." Ari was practically glowing. "But we didn't think you'd want to hear us gushing for fifteen minutes about how much we love and miss each other."

"Aww…" Dee pressed a hand to her chest.

"Eww," Tripp said. "Good call."

"Hater," Xavier chuckled.

"You two certainly look…cozy." Ari pursed her lips and batted her eyelashes. "Are you two at the breakfast stage of the relationship already?"

Ari giggled, endlessly amused, and Tripp shook his head, but grinned. Dee gasped, suddenly unable to speak. The only other person who seemed as disturbed by the implication of Ari's words was Xavier.

It looked like he'd sucked a whole lemon as his eyes narrowed at the screen in a message that seemed meant for Tripp.

"Relax, bro. Don't pop a blood vessel. Dee and I figured that taking the call together would allow us to immediately game-plan a few things afterward," Tripp said in an easy voice as he plucked the remaining piece of bacon from his plate and popped it into his mouth.

"Exactly." Dee nodded, finally finding her voice.

"So if everyone would refer to the agenda I emailed you."

Ari and Tripp both groaned.

"I see that you've been introduced to my incredibly organized best friend's love of spreadsheets and 'meeting'—" Ari used air quotes "—agendas."

"For which we're grateful." Xavier smiled. "We realize what an imposition this is for both of you, and we really appreciate you taking time out of your busy schedules to help us out."

This was exactly why Xavier had won her over. He was a genuinely good, kind and thoughtful guy. And so, it seemed, was his cousin.

"Okay, then," Dee said. "Here's what we're thinking…"

Eight

Tripp couldn't help smiling as he watched Dee gesticulate about the pros and cons of each option they were recommending. The woman was determined and focused whether she was discussing wedding venues or her favorite television show.

Normally, he'd considered anyone that impassioned about mundane matters to be a little too highstrung for his laid-back demeanor. But there was something about Dionna. She had a gift for getting others excited about things that might've seemed unimportant. And for making the most basic tasks seem fun and a bit exciting.

He wouldn't have believed it possible, but he was actually enjoying this whole wedding planning adventure with Dee. Not once had he felt the need to trot out the countless excuses he'd prepared in the event he felt the need to dip. And since he was as stubborn as she was, he was determined to make Dionna see how special Royal was.

"I love this point about intentionally selecting local vendors," Ex said. "Brilliant idea, Dee. This will generate excellent PR for the town and for us. And it'll create a lot of goodwill among the locals—including those who might be hesitant about the media circus this wedding is going to bring to their doorstep."

"Actually...that was all Tripp." Dionna gestured to him. "Honestly? I was against it initially. And while I realize there will need to be a couple of exceptions, now I can't help but agree. Utilizing local vendors is a good PR, logistic and financial move."

Tripp turned to Dee and winked, using the eye facing away from the camera. A secret gesture between just the two of them.

Dee took a sip of her ice water.

"You don't like the idea?" Dionna studied the worried look on her best friend's face.

"I do...*in theory*," Ari said carefully. "As long as Keely Tucker making my dress is one of those exceptions."

"Of course, I already told Tripp you'd want to work with Keely and your regular makeup artist, Lisette." Dee nodded. "Any other concerns?"

"You're sure this Seth Grayson is a top-rate photographer?" Ari's voice was filled with hesitation. "If he screws up our wedding photos... We'll never get the magic of that day back."

"Seth is a consummate professional and his work is always outstanding," Tripp assured the nervous bride-to-be.

"I was really impressed with Seth's portfolio. You'll find the link to it in the email. And you know I would never have cosigned this recommendation if I hadn't been blown away by his work." Dee offered her friend a reassuring smile. "Just wait until you see it."

"All right." Ari nodded, looking more at ease. "You know how much I value your opinion, Dee."

"I'll try not to take that personally." Tripp smirked.

"You know what I mean." Ari waved his comment off. "By the way, Mr. Connections, you wouldn't happen to have an award-winning makeup artist up your sleeve, would you? Because Lisette is expecting a baby around the same date as our wedding."

"Don't worry. I've got you," Tripp said.

"Don't tell me, you've got a personal makeup artist up your sleeve, too?" Ari marveled.

"Milan Valez is a makeup artist here in town. She works at the luxury spa PURE, and she does exceptional work. Her specialty is giving her clients a flawless finish without looking too made-up."

"You know an awful lot about makeup, cowboy," Dee noted.

"Milan did this incredible makeover for my sister when Tessa was the lone bachelorette in a charity auction at the Texas Cattleman's Club about five years ago. She's been booked solid ever since. So if you're interested, we'd better inquire about her availability right away," Tripp said. "Here. I'll drop her website link in the group text chat."

A moment later, everyone's phones dinged. There was silence as Dee and Ariana clicked on the link and scrolled to Milan's online portfolio.

"Milan does amazing work," Dee noted after scrolling through several photos.

"Have you seen the before and after photos? This woman is a freaking miracle worker." Ari looked up at the screen. "Tripp, please try to book Milan as soon as possible."

"Will do."

"After the wedding, we can have your publicist draw up a nice fluff piece about the wedding, naming all of the local vendors used." Dionna scanned her planner and notebook. "Unless anyone has something else, I think that covers everything."

"Actually, there is one other point I wanted to address," Tripp said. "When you'd planned to have the wedding in LA, you'd mentioned hosting a weeklong celebration with a variety of guest activities. Did you change your mind about that?"

"My plans were location-specific," Ari said as diplomatically as possible. "A visit to Disneyland, a film studio tour, whale watching, an evening cruise, a bonfire at the beach." She ticked the items off on her fingers.

"The events themselves would need to change, sure. But we can still have a week of prewedding festivities right here in Royal," Tripp said.

"That could be a lot of fun," Xavier agreed.

"This is the first I'm hearing about this." Dee peered at Tripp with one brow raised. A look that indicated they'd be having a *serious* talk after the call. "We haven't discussed any options, so I certainly can't weigh in on any recommendations. And I'm leaving tomorrow. There's no way I'll have time to help create and vet a weeklong agenda of guest activities."

Dee's in-control demeanor had shifted. She was flustered.

"Sorry, Dee." Tripp turned toward her, one hand pressed to her low back. "I didn't mean to throw you off. I just thought of this last night. That's why I came a few minutes early. I was hoping we could talk about it beforehand. But when I got here you were about to hop into the shower. I kind of forgot."

"Wait! You were there when Dee showered this morning?" Ari looked excited. "I need to hear more about this."

Dee flashed him a look that screamed *You had to say that right now?* Then she turned to the screen. "Tripp arrived earlier than we agreed. He sat in the living room and waited while I showered. Honestly, Ari, it's no big deal." Dee snapped her fingers. "Let's stay focused."

"Right. I need to leave for a speaking engagement in about forty minutes." Ex glanced down at the expensive watch on his wrist.

When Xavier looked up again, his expression contained a clear admonition: *Remember your promise, man. Do* not *fuck this up for me.*

Had the girls noticed Ex's warning look? If so, neither of them remarked on it.

"Tell us what you're thinking, Tripp," Ex continued.

"Most of the guests will be big city folks. So let's expose them to some fun things they wouldn't normally get to do," Tripp said.

"Like horseback riding or visiting a working ranch." Ex rubbed his chin and nodded. "I like it. What about you, babe?"

"I've kind of always wanted to visit a dude ranch and go horseback riding," Ari said excitedly.

"Ari, really?" Dee cocked her head. "I've never once heard you say you wanted to visit a dude ranch." Dionna folded her arms and stared at her friend incredulously. "You didn't even want to go bike riding a few weeks ago because you were afraid you'd break a nail."

"I know. But this sounds cool. Besides, I'm sure they have a nail salon there somewhere, right?" Ari giggled.

"Absolutely." Tripp had expected more pushback from Ariana.

"Won't you be sore after a day of dude ranching?" Dionna glared at Tripp. "Whatever that entails."

"Which is why we'll follow it up with a relaxing day of massages and pampering at PURE Spa here in town." A small smirk crept across Tripp's mouth when Dee's glare intensified.

"Brilliant idea, Tripp. I love it!" Ariana clapped excitedly. "But are there any other options for people who might not want to do something as vigorous as horseback riding or visiting a dude ranch?"

"Maybe a pottery or mosaic class at this really amazing antique shop in town, Priceless. And maybe Chef Colin or one of the other chefs in town might consider doing a cooking demo or something. And since you wanted a bonfire, we could end the week with an old-fashioned hayride and end the night with a bonfire party."

"Would there be line dancing involved?" Ari asked hopefully.

Tripp chuckled, glad the bride was on board. "You know it."

"This sounds amazing, babe," Ari said to Ex. "It would be a unique experience for our guests and a way to make our wedding stand out. What do you think?"

Xavier grinned. "I think we should do it."

"Great!" Ari said. "Sorry, Tripp. I hate to add more to your plate here. But would you mind working with Rylee to arrange the events?" Ariana held her hands together in prayer with pleading eyes.

"I'll get started on it as soon as possible."

"I'm thrilled that you're good with all of this." Dee's deep frown contradicted her words. "But there's no way I can fit all of this in before my plane takes off tomorrow."

"Which brings me to my second idea," Tripp said carefully. "I think Dee should stay a few more days. Maybe a week."

"What?" Dee turned to him, her eyes widening.

"That would give us time to figure all this out without being rushed," Tripp continued.

"I don't own my own ranch, mister," Dee reminded him. "I have a job to go back to."

"And as your employer," Ari said with a smile. "I would be totally okay with you working remotely for the next week or so. You don't have any big meetings at the office, right?"

"Well, no—"

"And we're still in the early stages of developing the cowboy story, right?" Ari continued.

"Well, yes—"

"Then this trip can add some insight to the project. Think of it as a research trip." Ari shrugged innocently.

Tripp could feel the tension rolling off Dee's shoulders.

Her eyes drifted closed for a micromoment. When she spoke again, she was as calm and logical as ever. "Ariana, this room costs a small fortune. Do we really need to pay for another week?"

"Which brings me to my third idea." Tripp focused on Ari's side of the screen and ignored the growing look of concern on Xavier's face. "Dee could stay in Tessa's old suite at the ranch. Got plenty of space, and it's just me rambling around that big old house now."

"I don't think Dee wants to—" Ex was saying.

"What a fantastic idea, Tripp," Ari said.

Dee turned to him. "You're suggesting I move in with you?"

"I'm inviting you to be my *guest* at The Noble

Spur," Tripp clarified. "The suite is like your own apartment, so you'll have plenty of private space. It even has an office."

"From what I've heard, it's a pretty big place," Ari said. "And with Tripp being out on the ranch during the day, it sounds like you'll have the place mostly to yourself, right?"

"Yes, ma'am." Tripp gave Dionna a reserved smile. "I can have the place prepped and ready for you by the time you check out tomorrow morning. So what do you say?"

Dee was still frowning. Her gaze shifted from his to Ari's.

Tripp refused to look at his cousin's side of the screen. And when his phone alerted him to a text message, he already knew it would be from Xavier. He discreetly set the phone on the table facedown without looking at the message.

"C'mon, Dee, it'll be fun. Besides, I told you there's a lot more to this town than you think. This will give me the chance to allay your concerns. What do you say?"

"Dee's not really the outdoors type. She's more board games and badminton," Ex interjected. "We shouldn't push her to do something outside of her comfort zone."

Dee's attention jerked to the screen. She folded her arms. "You're saying I'm a soft city girl who couldn't possibly handle life on a ranch for a week?"

"Uh-oh." Ari's expression made Tripp snort. "You're on your own with this one, partner."

"Of course not." Ex backpedaled. "I'm simply saying ranch life isn't your thing, and there's nothing wrong with that."

"I'm not asking Dee to come milk all our cows," Tripp said.

Xavier looked like he wanted to strangle him through the screen. "My point is you shouldn't make her feel obligated to—"

"I happen to be really good at milking cows."

"Xavier is right," Ari chimed in finally, casually filing a nail. "If Dee doesn't want to stay at Tripp's ranch, I can just put her up in the hotel for another week. I'm sure the room isn't that expensive."

"*Fine.* I'll do it," Dee said to Ari's side of the screen. She turned toward Tripp. "Okay, cowboy. You've got one week to convince me that Royal can be the Mecca of fun."

Tripp extended a hand and grinned. "You're on."

She slapped her palm against his a little too hard.

Tripp held back a chuckle. Maybe he was out of his skull. But it mattered to him what Dee thought of him and this little town. By the end of the week, he'd have Dionna Reed singing Royal's praises and wishing she could vacation here.

That's what this was about. Not about the fact that he looked forward to spending seven more days with her. Nope, that had nothing to do with this at all.

Nine

Dionna finished her call with one of the talent agents she often worked with, then sent what she hoped was her final email of the day. She shut her laptop, then glanced out of the window over the writing desk in what was once Tripp's sister Tessa's suite at The Noble Spur.

She couldn't help smiling.

The rolling plains, open fields and tree-lined creek were surprisingly beautiful and serene. For the first time in a really long time, it felt as if she could finally breathe—despite the flurry of calls and emails she'd waded through the past two days.

To be honest, after she'd gotten over the initial awkwardness of being in Tripp's home with his suite just down the hall from hers, being here had been...*nice*.

She'd forgotten how peaceful it was to be in a place where people didn't live on top of one another. Where she wasn't forced to battle grueling traffic daily. Dionna walked into the attached bedroom and out onto the small balcony. It was late February. Yet, the temperatures were in the midsixties, and beneath the glare of the sun it felt even warmer.

Dee closed her eyes and soaked in the sun's rays. She took a deep breath. The air was pure and exhilarating. And except for the occasional conversation that drifted her way when a few of the ranch hands passed by, it was quiet. She could hear herself think, a luxury she hadn't been afforded in so long.

"Afternoon, Miss Dee." Roy Jensen, one of the ranch hands, removed his hat and wiped the sweat from his brow with his sleeve before settling his lovingly worn Stetson back onto his head. "Mighty pretty day, ain't it?"

"Please call me Dee." Her smile widened as she glanced around. "And it certainly is."

They chatted briefly, then the older man was on his way. Roy reminded Dee of her grandfather back when she'd spent summers on their farm. Roy Jensen and every other person she'd encountered in Royal seemed so warm and *genuine*.

Tripp had introduced her to several of the locals when they ate lunch at The Royal Diner earlier in the day. It was a quaint little 1950s throwback-style diner with chrome stools, red faux-leather booths and a black-and-white checkerboard floor. Something about just stepping into the place had made her instantly giddy.

Her grandmother always said she was an old soul born in the wrong era. Maybe Grandma Elaine was right.

Because despite all the unexpected modern touches, in some ways being here in Royal felt like stepping back in time to a simpler, quieter life. A life she hadn't realized that she'd missed. Not that she'd ever considered moving out to her grandparents' farm full-time. But those wondrous summers she'd spent with them were cathartic and refreshing. They prepared her for another school year and the stress of being the odd-ball teenage girl living in LA and attending classes with the *cool kids*. She'd been a square peg that hadn't even attempted to fit into the round holes her fellow students happily occupied.

At the diner, unlike in LA, no one tried to pitch her a script to pass on to her famous bestie Ariana. They were more impressed that Ariana seemed like a sweet girl and that she and Xavier always looked so happy whenever they were on the red carpet. And they all seemed to appreciate Ari's gesture of moving the wedding to her fiancé's hometown. It made them even more endearing.

Dionna was beginning to see why Tripp loved Royal so much.

She stepped back inside and closed the sliding glass door. She was startled by the doorbell. As far as she knew, Tripp was still out on the ranch surveying some of their unused land. Land that had originally been allotted to Xavier's family.

And since Tripp's part-time housekeeper had left about an hour ago, leaving a savory beef stew simmering in the Crock-Pot, Dee was the only one in the house.

It felt odd answering Tripp's door when he wasn't there. But when the bell rang again, she made her way down the stairs.

"Yes?" She smiled at the tall, lanky young man.

"Delivery," the boy said. "Should I sit it down inside? The box is kind of heavy."

"Sure. I guess." Dee permitted him to set the box just inside the door. "Tripp isn't here right now, but I can sign for it, if you need me to."

The boy's eyes finally met hers. "These aren't for Tripp. You're—" he studied the small black pad "—Dionna Reed, right?" When she nodded, he extended the pad. "Great. Sign here."

Dee thanked him, then closed the door. She hoisted the heavy box up to her room.

"I swear to God, if Ari sent me lingerie, I'm going to strangle her," Dee muttered under her breath.

Her best friend had been teasing her endlessly about her and Tripp making a good couple. She'd been particularly sensitive to Ari's gentle ribbing because the more she'd gotten to know Tripp, the more she actually *did* like him. Not that anything was going to happen between them.

Tripp had been a perfect gentleman. And as much

as she hated to admit it, a small part of her was disappointed by that.

Aside from their meals together and their wedding planning field trips, Tripp had given Dee her space. During the day, she had the house to herself mostly.

Does Tripp ever get lonely in this big old house all alone?

Given how well he knew the layout of The Bellamy and its suites, the answer was probably no.

Still, she couldn't help thinking back to when she'd first arrived.

"Aren't all ranchers supposed to have a dog?" Dee had teased. "A Saint Bernard isn't going to come rushing out and tackle me, is it?"

Tripp's features had pinched. He'd shoved his hands in his pockets. "My last dog, Ace... We lost him about a year ago." He'd shrugged. "I was more broken up about it than my niece." He'd tapped a hand on his chest. "Don't think I have the capacity to go through that again just yet."

If she hadn't already been into the guy, that moment would've made her fall for him instantly.

Dee grabbed some scissors from the desk and opened the box.

The clothes inside weren't hers this time. But she doubted they were from Ari either. Definitely not her friend's style.

The prices had been removed, but the sales tags indicated that everything in the box had come from The Rancher's Daughter, one of the shops Tripp had taken her to the previous day prior to dining at a restaurant called The Eatery.

She examined the contents of the box. Saddle-brown canvas work pants with loads of pockets. A pair of bootcut jeans with a star stitched on the back pocket, that had fit her body like a glove when she'd tried them on in the store. Distressed ankle-length jeans frayed at the hem that she'd admired on the rack. Button-down plaid rodeo shirts in a variety of color combinations. The gorgeous cowboy boots she'd tried on.

Dionna lifted a tall, studded brown boot from the box, inhaling the scent of the leather and admiring the turquoise-colored sole. She ran her fingers over the gorgeous stitching: a mythological firebird embroidered with tan thread.

The boots were stunning and surprisingly comfortable. Like they'd been made for her. But they were also expensive. And since they didn't exactly mesh with her white shirt and black pants LA wardrobe, she'd left them in the store.

So why were they here now?

Dee reached for the card at the bottom of the box, which bore her name. She flipped it over.

Gear up for our ride tomorrow. No more excuses.

The card was signed by Tripp.

He bought me clothing?

For the past two days, he'd asked her to go riding with him. She'd begged off, saying she hadn't brought appropriate clothing. Maybe next time.

Well, Mr. Problem Solver had apparently solved

her little problem. But she couldn't believe he'd shelled out the amount of money he had just to get her to go horseback riding with him. And she certainly couldn't accept such an expensive gift. She would thank him and then politely return everything.

Dee held up the jeans that had made her ass look incredible.

Maybe I'll keep these... But I'll pay for them myself.

She picked up the boot again and looked at it longingly. Maybe she wasn't going to go home with them. But would it hurt if she tried them on again? Then again, to get the full effect, she should probably try on the entire outfit. She'd snap a couple of mirror selfies to send to Ari. Then she'd pack everything up and send it back to The Rancher's Daughter along with her apologies for the misunderstanding.

Still, she couldn't help being moved by how generous Tripp had been.

Tripp stepped out of a hot shower, his muscles already starting to ache. It had been a long time since he'd helped bale hay and mend fences, but a couple of his ranch hands had fallen ill, and they'd been shorthanded that day. He'd rediscovered a few muscles he'd apparently been missing in his weekly workouts. Experience told him the following day would be much worse.

Tripp shrugged on a pair of his favorite broken-in jeans, tugged on a black T-shirt and headed down the hall to check on Dee. The entire house smelled of savory beef stew, and he was starving. Hopefully, Dee was ready to eat, too.

The door was partially open, but Tripp knocked anyway, startling Dee. She was modeling the clothing he'd had sent over from Morgan Grandin's shop, The Rancher's Daughter.

"Tripp!" Dee whipped around. "What are you, part cat? I didn't realize you were home."

The look on her face reminded him of when Tessa had gotten busted wearing half of their mother's makeup when she was about five. He reined in a grin.

"I got here about a half an hour ago. It was a tough day. I needed a long hot shower." Tripp leaned against the door, taking her in. Dee was wearing those jeans that looked like they'd been tailored to her body with its mesmerizing curves, one of the rodeo shirts and the boots she'd fallen in love with at the store. He rubbed his chin and nodded approvingly. "You look amazing in that outfit, and it fits perfectly."

"You really think so?" She faced the mirror again, giving him a prize view of her...*assets.*

Don't even think about it.

He repeated the words in his head, but Dee was all he'd been able to think about for the past week. More so since he'd had the genius idea to invite her to stay at The Noble Spur.

"Sweetheart, I have eyes," he said. The term of endearment had slipped out without thought.

Dee seemed surprised by it but didn't object. Her gaze met his, reflected in the mirror. She cleared her throat and turned to face him. "Thank you for this incredibly thoughtful gift, Tripp." She gestured toward the open box sitting on the trunk at the foot of the bed. "But I can't accept it."

"Why not?" Tripp kept his voice neutral. "I've gifted you things before."

"This isn't a bouquet of flowers or lunch at the diner, Tripp. It's an entire freaking wardrobe." She glanced down at the clothing she was wearing, seemingly frustrated that he didn't seem to understand the difference between the two.

He did. Didn't mean he wouldn't downplay it anyway.

"You needed some ranch gear. It's a few pairs of pants and a few shirts. Not a big deal," Tripp said.

"Yes, but everything here was pretty pricey. Those boots alone cost nearly six hundred dollars." She extended her leg, showing off the vibrant turquoise sole of her boot. When he didn't respond, she crossed the room and stood a few feet in front of him, her soft spring scent filling his nostrils. "This was really thoughtful of you, Tripp. But—"

"Honestly, Dee, it's fine. I've blown money on things far more frivolous. If it helps, don't think of this as a gift. Think of it as me being a selfish bastard dead set on getting what I want."

"Which is…"

You. Right here. Right now.

He willed the voice inside his head that was way too fucking honest to shut up.

"For you to go horseback riding with me," he finally managed. "It'll be fun."

"Tripp…"

"That's why you stayed another week, right? To get a feel for the prewedding events I'm proposing. So we can make a decision on them before you leave next Sunday."

Why did those last words catch in his throat?

He couldn't keep Dee here with him forever. But it had been nice having company in the house again. And he'd enjoyed the time they'd spent together exploring Royal as they helped plan the wedding and shared meals all over town.

He hadn't realized how much he'd missed the company. Maybe this wasn't about Dee at all. Maybe he'd become a hermit and he just needed to get back out there again, date, and be social.

Tripp studied Dee's face as she debated her response.

You're full of it, and you know it.

This was definitely about Dionna. He wasn't lonely for just any company. He enjoyed *her* company.

"Yes, that's why I stayed," Dee said finally, shaking Tripp from his thoughts. "But I could rent a car and drive to a big-box store in Dallas. I'm pretty sure the horses won't mind if I'm not wearing designer gear and a pair of six-hundred-dollar boots." The slow smile that spread across her face made her dark eyes twinkle and tugged at something in his chest.

"I don't know." Tripp shrugged, taking a couple steps closer, leaving a foot of space between them. "Deuce and Nick Fury have *pretty* discriminating tastes."

Dionna dissolved into laughter. The joyous sound filled the room and made his heart dance.

When their laughter had died down, Tripp placed a hand on Dee's shoulder. "Seriously, Dee, you look amazing, and I want you to have this stuff. I'm a bachelor with zero responsibilities and very few vices other than spoiling my niece and nephew. So let me do this."

Dee cocked her head. "On one condition."

He'd never found it quite so difficult to gift a woman with anything before. "Name it."

"Tell me why it's so important for you to convince me of how great Royal is?"

Tripp dropped his hand from her shoulder. There was an intensity in Dee's eyes. Telling her anything other than the truth wasn't an option. If there was one thing he'd learned about Dionna Reed, it was that the woman was a walking, talking bullshit detector.

He scrubbed a hand down his face and sighed. "Because maybe I care what you think."

"Hmm." Dee sized him up. "The way Xavier tells it, you're this badass rebel who doesn't care what anyone thinks."

"And that's true." He shrugged. *Mostly.*

Dee inched closer. "Then why do you care what I think of Royal or you, Tripp?"

The room felt hot and a little claustrophobic. He searched his brain for anything he could tell her. Anything other than the truth. He came up empty.

"Because your opinion matters to me, Dee. So what

you think of the place that made me who I am and that I call home matters to me, too."

"Why?" Dee's voice was barely more than a whisper. There was a hunger in her gaze that he knew well. One he'd promised himself he wouldn't give into.

"Because I like you, Dionna. A lot." The words scraped at Tripp's throat like tiny shards of glass. Yet, he felt a sense of relief once he'd finally uttered them.

"What if I said I like you, too, Tripp?"

Tripp's gaze dropped to her full lips. His brain was suddenly overwhelmed with imagining the taste and feel of those lush lips.

Dee's chest rose and fell with shallow breaths as she awaited his response.

He tried to summon his cousin's plea for him not to mess things up for him. But Ex's voice was tinny and distant. Imperceptible over the sound of his own heart thundering in his chest.

Tripp closed the space between them, his lips crashing into Dee's. One arm slid around her waist, tugging her body against his. The other hand cradled her cheek, angling Dee's head as his lips glided over hers.

Warmth filled his chest and trailed down his spine. And when Dee wrapped her arms around his waist, as if she desperately needed the contact between them, he thought he might combust from the sensation of his growing length pressed hard into her belly.

Dee slid her hands beneath his T-shirt. She traced the damp skin on his back with her fingertips, then lightly grazed it with her short nails.

Dee's lips parted, and Tripp nibbled on her lush

lower lip, evoking a soft gasp. He glided his tongue between her lips, swallowing the soft murmurs that made him increasingly hard. Hungrier for the taste of her mouth. The taste of her skin. Desperate to know what sounds she would make when he slid inside her. Or when he drove her over the edge. When she fell apart beneath him.

Tripp tightened his arm around Dee's waist. He pressed his other hand to her back as he ravaged her mouth—sweet and warm. Tasting of chocolate and mint. In that moment, there was nothing he wanted more than to strip every single piece of clothing from her body and taste the soft brown skin that had teased him from the moment he'd laid eyes on Dee in that little black minidress the day she'd first arrived in Royal.

Suddenly, Dee pulled back. Her chest heaving as her teeth sank into her lower lip. Her eyes searched his.

Tripp swallowed hard, still holding on to Dee as they both caught their breath. When she didn't speak, he opened his mouth to apologize. To tell her he hadn't intended to kiss her. Even as he realized he wasn't sorry at all that he had.

"Dee, I—"

Dionna grasped the hem of his T-shirt, and he helped her tug it over his head. She tossed it onto the floor.

Tripp's heart pounded against his rib cage as she dipped her head and pressed a kiss to his chest. Then another and another. When she gazed up at him again, he could clearly see the desire that was likely reflected in his own eyes.

Every ounce of control he'd been wearing like a suit of armor for the past few days had been weakened by that look in her eyes. It'd crumbled and turned to dust at his feet.

Tripp kissed Dee as if hers was the last kiss he'd ever need. His hands fumbled with the snaps on her shirt, ripping them open. He tugged the garment off and dropped it into the box it came from. He unclasped her bra and slid it from her arms, taking a moment to appreciate the full round breasts he'd been imagining for the past week. He grazed the dark brown peaks with his calloused thumb, eager for a taste.

He palmed Dee's deliciously curvy ass and lifted her. She hooked her legs around his back as he carried her to the bed a few yards away. He deposited her there, and together they tugged off the jeans that fit her like a second skin.

"Shit," Tripp muttered. "I need to grab a condom." *Or three.* "Don't move. I'll be right back."

A smile spread across Dee's gorgeous face. She nodded.

Tripp sprinted to his end of the hall and grabbed a strip of condoms from his nightstand before hurrying back.

Dee was beneath the covers smiling. She'd let her hair down, her dark brown twists spread across the pillow. And the last garment she'd been wearing—a lacy pair of black underwear—had been discarded onto the floor.

Tripp quickly shed his remaining clothing and sheathed himself before climbing beneath the covers. He reveled in the sensation of her soft bare skin gliding against his as he kissed her. And he loved the way the hardened brown peaks poked at his chest, and the thrill of his painfully hard dick nestled between their bellies.

He loved the soft murmurs that emanated from her throat as their kiss heated up. Especially when he rolled off of Dee and glided his hand up her leg.

"Oh God, Tripp," Dee murmured against his lips when his fingers reached the warm, wet space between her thighs.

He couldn't help thinking that he'd do just about anything to hear her utter those words again in that breathy tone that made him so hard he ached with the need to be inside her.

Tripp watched her expression, eyes shuttered, as he slipped two fingers inside her and grazed her clit with his thumb. He wasn't even inside her yet, and already he was addicted to every little sound she made. And the way she whispered his name desperately again and again.

He covered one of her stiffened nipples with his mouth, sucking it and teasing it with his tongue. Grazing it gently with his teeth. Loving how her pleasure continued to spiral beneath his touch. He moved to the other nipple, then trailed kisses down her body, his fingers still working as he slipped yet another inside of her.

When he sucked her clit into his mouth, she cursed and lifted her hips, silently begging for more. He loved the salty sweet taste of her. The way she whimpered his name as her legs and belly stiffened and her body shuddered around his fingers.

Tripp pressed soft kisses to her quivering flesh. Then he kissed his way back up her belly before kissing her neck and jaw as her breathing slowed.

Dee sucked in a deep breath, then opened her eyes. She smiled at him almost shyly.

He couldn't remember the last time someone had looked at him that way. Or made him feel as possessive as he felt about her now. Like he couldn't bear the thought of her gifting that incredible smile to anyone else. Because he wanted it all for himself.

Tripp swallowed hard. Tried not to think about the implications of that statement. Or all of the reasons he shouldn't feel so deeply for a woman who'd be gone in a few days and lived thousands of miles away.

Instead, he gripped his hardened length, pumping it a few times before pressing it against her slick entrance. He closed his eyes, reveling in her soft whimpers and the way her nails grazed his back as he inched inside her until he was fully seated.

Was she just as titillated by the muffled groans that escaped his throat as her body swallowed his?

Dee wrapped her legs around him, her bare heels pressing into the small of his back, as he moved inside her. He circled his hips, his pelvis grounding against the bundle of nerves. Evoking increasingly intense murmurs of pleasure every time he made contact with it again.

Tripp's arms trembled slightly, supporting most of his weight as he increased his speed and intensity. Until Dee's back arched and she practically screamed his name. A few more thrusts of his hips, and he let the pulsing of her body pull him over the edge.

He tumbled onto his back and heaved a sigh, his chest rising and falling. Tripp wrapped his arms around Dionna and cradled her to his chest. Their heavy breathing, nearly in sync, were the only sounds in the room.

Tripp pushed a few of the long twists off her face and kissed her forehead. Inhaled the coconut and vanilla scent of her hair that he'd come to crave.

"That was…amazing, Dee." Tripp glided his hand up and down her back, loving the feel of her soft bare skin.

"It was, wasn't it?" Dionna flashed him her shy smile again, one hand pressed to his chest. She snuggled against him and sighed contentedly, like there was no place in the world she'd rather be. After a few more minutes of silence, she said, "Xavier made you promise not to make a move on me, didn't he?"

Tripp wasn't surprised she'd deduced as much. Not after the evil eye Ex had given him during their video chat.

"He did, and I probably deserve to get my ass kicked

for this," Tripp admitted. "But the only thing I regret is having made the promise in the first place."

Dee looked up at him and smiled, like it was exactly what she needed to hear.

Tripp kissed her, then excused himself for a trip to the bathroom. Then he slipped back into bed. He'd never considered himself a cuddler. But lying in bed with Dee's cheek pressed to his chest and her arms wrapped around him... He couldn't deny that it felt *nice*. He'd gladly fall asleep to the sound of her breathing as he held her in his arms.

"Hello! Tripp, we're here!" a familiar voice called.

Shit.

Tripp glanced at the Asorock watch on his wrist with its leather band and rose-gold case. Time had gotten away from him.

Dionna lifted onto one arm, her brows scrunching as she pulled the sheet up around her. "Is that your parents?"

"My sister. I forgot that Tess invited herself and her family over for dinner tonight. Their cook is on vacation, and Marguerite's beef stew is one of Tess's favorite meals."

"This is her old room. She isn't coming up here, is she?" Dionna glanced toward the partially open door.

"Not if I cut her off first." Tripp pressed a quick kiss to Dee's lips. He climbed out of bed, shrugged on his boxers and jeans, then called down to his sister. "Hey, Tess. Can you set up the table? Dee and I both took naps before dinner. I'll wake her and then we'll both be down shortly."

There was a long pregnant pause. "Sure. No problem."

He could tell his sister wasn't buying his story. But no need to alarm Dee. She'd put on her underwear and was searching the floor on her hands and knees, presumably for her bra.

"What a spectacular view."

"What?" Dee glanced up at him, looking irritated.

"No need to panic. I'll stall them with my sparkling conversation." He retrieved her bra from beneath the bed, then helped her up. He kissed her again. "Besides, we're unattached adults. We can do whatever the hell we want."

"We're adults who'd prefer to keep this to ourselves," she reminded him, her eyes pleading.

"Got it." Tripp nodded. But if he knew his sister, keeping this a secret was a ship that had already sailed.

Ten

Dionna stood in her underwear staring at the jeans, shirt and cowboy boots she'd hastily discarded. Her hands shook as she debated whether or not to put them back on.

Dee shrugged on the jeans, one of her own shirts and a pair of socks. Then she stuffed her feet into the slippers Tripp had loaned her and went to the bathroom to pin her wild, just-tumbled-out-of-bed hair back up into a sensible bun. The kind of hairdo that said, "I *wasn't* upstairs screwing your brother just now... *Really.*"

She wiped off her smeared tinted lip gloss so she could reapply it. Once she was satisfied she didn't look like she'd just gotten done banging the woman's brother, she placed her hand on the doorknob of the now closed door. She froze in place, her hands still shaking.

Dee was a terrible liar. Tessa would know something was up the moment she laid eyes on her.

"We are so busted." Dee leaned her head against the door.

Her cell phone rang, and she retrieved it from the desk. Molly Hawthorne, the talent agent, was calling her back.

Something work-related. This, she could handle.

"Hey, Molly. What's up?"

Nothing happening here. Really!

"Sweetie, are you okay? You sound like you just ran up a flight of stairs?" Molly said.

"I was working out." Not a lie…*exactly.* That was certainly the best workout she'd gotten in a long time. "But I'm sure you didn't call to discuss my exercise routine. What's going on?"

"Marcus Maybury is *definitely* interested in this role of a badass Black cowboy fighting to hold on to his land!" Molly squealed. "But you know how Marcus is. He's all about authenticity. He wants to know if a consultant will be on set to ensure that the movie comes off as being completely credible. And he isn't interested in making some green screen Western. He'll only consider the project if you're filming on an actual ranch—not on some studio lot."

"I see." Dionna rolled her eyes, hoping her tone didn't reflect her earnest feelings about Marcus's request. "Well, we certainly appreciate how dedicated he is to his craft."

Marcus's star was steadily rising in Hollywood. And he'd be the biggest star that Ariana's fledgling studio had snagged thus far. Her best friend had been adamant that they should do whatever it took to book Marcus for this movie—their most ambitious film to date. But filming on-site, God knows where, and hiring a consultant? Who was this guy to dictate such terms?

Would he be throwing his limited weight around if they had been a larger studio? Or one headed up by a male actor instead?

Dee tried to push aside her personal objections. Her job was to execute Ari's wishes for the project. And what Ari wanted was to secure Marcus Maybury for the lead role in this movie.

"We're certainly willing to entertain both requests," Dee said as she stared out onto Tripp's property.

"Excellent, because he's deciding between this project and two others." Molly switched from hard-nosed negotiator to Valley Girl cheerleader in three seconds flat. "He'll want to know where you'll be filming. What should I tell him?"

"Uhh…" Dionna hadn't expected to have to come up with an answer right away—before she got the chance to speak to Ari about it. If she didn't come up with a satisfactory answer, Marcus would walk.

"Well?" Molly's tone indicated that she had the feeling Dee was bullshitting.

Suddenly, the answer was right in front of her. Dee stood tall, her gaze sweeping the rolling plains she'd been admiring the past few days. "I'm scouting a possible site right now. It's a gorgeous sprawling ranch in Royal, Texas, that happens to be owned by fourth-generation Black ranchers."

"Talk about authentic," Molly said, almost reverently. "So I assume the owners will be your consultants—to ensure the movie feels authentic."

"That's what we're hoping." Dee palmed her forehead and cringed.

What on earth was I thinking?

"Fantastic! If you can nail down this location and the consultant, I can pretty much assure you Marcus will be on board with the project. We both feel this could be that breakout role he's been searching for. Get back to me as soon as you can, doll."

Dee paced the floor, her head throbbing.

Now all she had to do was convince the man she'd just slept with to agree to it. Before she'd even had a chance to process what had happened between them.

Tripp had undoubtedly expected their little tryst to be a no-strings-attached encounter. But now she needed to ask him to let them film on his property for several weeks.

It sounded like the kind of request that would make an unattached playboy like Tripp Noble panic, thinking she wanted something more. She just needed to assure him that she didn't. Even if, in her heart, she already knew she did.

"Hey, sis." Tripp hugged his sister, then kissed the forehead of his six-month-old nephew, Dylan, perched on her hip. The infant offered him a gurgle and a gummy grin of recognition. "Sorry, we were short-handed today. I had to be a lot more hands-on than I'm used to. Needed a hot shower and a quick nap. Time got away from me."

"And was your houseguest baling hay, too? Is that why she also needed a *nap*?" His sister didn't do the dreaded air quotes, but the way she'd said *nap* said it well enough.

"My guess? She's had a pretty taxing day, too."

"I see." Tess switched Dylan—a rather solid infant—to her other hip. "But that doesn't really explain *this*—" Tess motioned around her mouth "—now does it?"

Tessa produced a tissue from her pocket.

Shit. Dionna had been wearing a colored lip gloss.

"Is this thing clean?" Tripp raised an eyebrow.

"Of course!" Tessa popped his arm. "And I assume we'll talk about this later."

Tripp wiped his mouth without committing to anything. He stuffed the tissue in his pocket and turned toward his brother-in-law and young niece who'd entered through the door off the kitchen.

"What's up, Ryan?" Tripp slapped palms with his brother-in-law. Then he swept his three-year-old niece off her feet and tossed her in the air.

Tiana squealed with delight.

"Be careful, you two," Tessa pleaded.

"Hey, Tee! How is Uncle Tripp's favorite niece in the whole wide world?" Tripp tickled the little girl's belly.

She giggled, wriggling in his arms.

"Daddy took me to say hello to Deuce and Nick Fury," Tiana declared, once she finally got her giggles under control.

"You did?" His niece loved horses. "Well, that was nice of you. Did you take them a treat?"

"Mmm-hmm." The little girl nodded vigorously. "Daddy let me give them apples."

"One thing I know about Deuce and Nick is that they love a woman bearing gifts. So good job." Tripp kissed the little girl's cheek, then set her on her feet. He gently tugged one of her braids, accented with colorful beads. "Ready for dinner?"

"I'm famished." Tiana pressed the back of her hand to her head dramatically.

"Famished?" Tripp eyed his sister. "Have you been reading her the dictionary at bedtime?"

Ryan slipped an arm around Tessa's waist, both of them laughing.

"Blame our mother for that one and for the dramatics," Tess said. "Tee picked it up from some old black-and-white movie she was watching with Mom before they left for their trip to Cuba with Xavier's parents."

"Figures," Tripp chuckled. Their mother, once an aspiring actress who yearned to be cast in cowboy movies, had ended up marrying one instead. Tripp squeezed the little girl's shoulder. "All right, Little Miss Famished. We'll be eating soon. So you'd better go wash your hands."

Tiana didn't need to be told twice. She took off toward the first-floor powder room as fast as her legs would carry her.

"We can't start dinner without the guest of honor." Tessa handed Dylan to Ryan. "Should I go check on her?"

"No, nosy." Tripp raised an eyebrow.

"Sorry to have kept you waiting. I had to take an important call." Dee made her way down the stairs. "You must be Tripp's sister, Tessa. I'm Dionna Reed, a friend of Ariana and Xavier's. It's a pleasure to finally meet you." Dee extended a hand.

"It's a pleasure to finally meet you, too." Tess bypassed Dee's hand and wrapped her up in a hug. "I feel like I already know you. Tripp has told me so much about you."

"Same." Dee seemed pleasantly surprised by the hug.

Tessa introduced Dionna to her husband and their children. They chatted about the wedding and some of the shops and eateries Dionna had visited around town while she helped Tess prepare everyone's plates.

By the time they settled around the dinner table, Dee seemed more relaxed, the tension melting from her shoulders.

He liked having Dionna here. She got along well with his family. His niece and nephew gravitated toward her, and Dee was incredibly patient with them.

Tripp tried to play it cool. But he often caught himself sneaking glances at her. Touching her whenever he could manufacture a plausible reason to do so, even if it was something as simple as leaning his leg against hers beneath the dinner table.

They played a few games after dinner and ended the

night with a round of spades and ice cream sandwiches made from Dee's homemade chocolate chip cookies and filled with Neapolitan ice cream—Tessa's favorite.

"It's been a lovely evening." Dionna stood after she and Tripp beat Tessa and Ryan handily in a game of spades. "But there are a few emails I need to send before I head to bed. It was such a pleasure meeting your lovely family, Tess and Ryan. I hope I get to see you all again before I leave."

"The pleasure was all ours." Tessa stood, with Dylan on her hip, and wrapped Dee in a one-arm hug. "And if my brother doesn't keep you hidden away here at the house… He never did like to share—" Tess added in a mock whisper. "Then we'll definitely see you again before you leave."

"Looking forward to it." Dee's smile was so sweet and genuine. He couldn't help smiling, too. "Tripp, don't worry about the dishes. I'll clean up as soon as I've sent my emails."

"Absolutely not," Tess insisted. "You're a guest."

Tripp tipped his chin toward the stairs. "Like Tess said, we've got it."

Dee waved good-night, then headed upstairs.

"I should get the kids home, give them baths and get them to bed." Ryan stood.

"But I'm not sleepy, Daddy." Tee yawned. "I want to help Mommy and Uncle Tripp clean up."

"Next time, pudding." Ryan squatted and kissed his daughter's cheek. "Tonight, I need your help giving your baby brother a bath. Think you can help your old man out?"

"Yes, Daddy." Tiana gave her father a sleepy smile. She kissed her mother and Tripp good-night.

Tripp and Tessa carried the dessert dishes into the kitchen, and Tess began rinsing them.

Tripp pulled out the dishwasher rack and loaded the dishes as his sister handed them to him. "All right, Tess. What is it that you want to talk about?"

"It should be pretty obvious what we need to talk about."

"I'm a grown-ass, bill-paying adult," he reminded her. "We don't *need* to talk about anything."

"True. But let's just say we will anyway. Not because you owe me an explanation. Because I care about you and Xavier, and I really like Dee. I don't want to see anyone get hurt." Tessa kept rinsing dishes and handing them to him.

"What makes you think I'll hurt Dee?" Tripp's jaw tensed. "You're my sister. You should know me better than that."

Tessa turned off the water and faced him. "I do know you, Tripp. I realize you wouldn't intentionally hurt anyone. That doesn't mean that you don't leave people hurt in your wake. Face it, big brother, you're a lovable guy. So maybe it's easy for you to walk away. That isn't necessarily so for the other party."

Tripp frowned. "Are we talking about anyone in particular?"

"It doesn't matter." Tessa sounded sad. "The point is just because you don't mean to hurt someone, it doesn't mean they won't end up hurt. And in this

case, there's a lot at stake. Isn't that why you promised Ex you wouldn't—"

"Ex called you about this?"

"You stopped answering his calls."

Touché.

"Okay, I shouldn't have done that," he admitted.

"Nor should you have made him a promise you
had no intention of keeping," Tess scolded.

"The way Ryan did when he promised he'd never
lay a hand on my little sister?" Tripp glared at her.

"That was different." Tess glared right back. "First,
you two had no right making such an agreement on
my behalf. Second, yes, you and Ryan were close
friends, but he and I had an established friendship."
Tessa ticked off each point on her fingers.

"Same on both counts."

Tessa rolled her eyes. "Ryan and I have been friends
since we were kids. It isn't the same, Tripp."

"Maybe we haven't known each other as long. But
we have been steadily building a friendship over the
past few months… Before she came to town," he reminded her.

"Ryan and I were willing to take the risk because
we truly cared for each other. We could imagine having a life together. The risk was worth the reward."
Tess's frustration showed in the creases between her
brows. "Can you say the same?"

"Maybe." The word flew out of Tripp's mouth before he could stop it. It shocked them both into silence.

He leaned against the old butcher-block countertop and shrugged. "I don't know."

"You've *never* said that before about *anyone*." Tessa was still stunned.

"I know."

"Wow." Tessa leaned against the countertop, too. "But you've really only known each other for like a week," Tessa noted. "Or have you been crushing this hard on her all along and just tried to be chill about it?"

"I'm a little old for crushes." He folded his arms and crossed one ankle over the other. "But was I into her since before she arrived here? I guess. More than I realized, apparently."

Tessa's brows furrowed in thought. He could tell she was thinking hard about what to say.

"Have you considered maybe the reason it feels safe to fall for Dionna is because (a) she's not anything like the women you typically go for and (b) the relationship feels…impossible."

"I think that her not being my usual type is, surprisingly, what I like most about her." Tripp smiled fondly, then turned to his sister and frowned. "Wait… Why do you think the relationship feels impossible? I'd think that you and Mom would be thrilled that I'm considering getting serious about someone."

"I've never pressured you about settling down. I trust that when you find the right person, you will."

"How do you know Dee isn't that person?" Tripp asked.

"You live in Royal and run this ranch. Your life

is tied to this land and to this town. Dee is a Hollywood casting director. Therefore, her life is tied to LA. Surely, this isn't news to you." Tess laid a gentle hand on his arm and sighed. "I really do like Dee. I'd love it if she was The One. But I just don't see how you two could ever make that work without one of you giving up a huge part of who you are. Do you?"

Tripp rubbed his chin and sighed.

He didn't have a response to that. And maybe Tess was right. Maybe feeling this way about Dee felt safe because there were so many obstacles to overcome.

"You're right. Our lives and livelihoods are tied to specific geographic locations thousands of miles apart." He met Tess's gaze. "But I do feel something for her."

Tess slipped her arm through his and leaned her head on his shoulder. "I wish I had some brilliant solution."

"Me too." The words caused a deep ache in Tripp's chest.

Tessa turned to face him. "You know, if you ever decide that running the ranch isn't what you want, I'd understand."

"Thanks, sis." He gestured to the tattoo on her arm. The same Noble Spur brand in the same place on her forearm as his. Something they'd done together a few weeks before Tessa got married. "But this place is in my blood, same as yours. It'll always be home."

The fact was, Dee would be walking out of his life soon and he had no alternative to offer her. It was a reality he wasn't prepared to accept.

Eleven

Dee paced her room at The Noble Spur, her heart racing and her head spinning. She'd had to set what had happened between her and Tripp aside while they had dinner with his sister and brother-in-law and pretended that nothing had happened between them. But it had. And she hadn't been able to stop thinking about it and about Tripp.

She'd left the dinner table more than an hour earlier. And she'd watched Ryan walk the kids back over to their place next door—Bateman Ranch. When she'd ventured out of her suite, she could hear Tripp's and Tessa's voices downstairs. She couldn't hear what they were saying, but she couldn't help thinking that she was the subject of the conversation.

They'd insisted that they were just friends. But so

many times during the evening, she could feel the heat of Tripp's stare warming her skin. She'd been grateful that her dark brown skin tone camouflaged the flush of her skin whenever he'd placed a hand on her back or grazed her knee with his beneath the table.

Her skin had run hot, and a zap of electricity ran along the surface and shot down her spine. She'd barely been able to look at him without reliving the moments they'd shared in this room. Even now, she could practically feel his soft lips caressing her skin. His calloused fingers exploring her body and taking her to heights she hadn't known.

Dionna stood in the mostly dark room, lit only by the lamp on the desk, as she stared out of the balcony window.

What have you done, Dionna Reed?

She ran her fingers through her twists and sighed. The moments between them had been absolute magic. Everything she could've hoped for and more. But she'd also screwed things up, hadn't she?

Because Tripp Noble was clearly not the kind of man you got serious about. She'd gone into this well aware of that. Still, she couldn't stop herself. And she hadn't wanted to. But what she was feeling for him right now... This was about more than Tripp being charming and amazing in bed.

They'd gotten to know each other a little through their online interactions. At first, it had been easy to dismiss her growing feelings for Tripp as a silly crush. But the time they'd spent together the past few days had shown her a different side of Tripp. Made her believe that there was so much more to him than the charming jokester he showed to the world. And she felt such a deep attraction to the man. The thought of walking away in a few days and pretending none of this had ever happened made her heart ache for whatever might have been.

It was silly. She realized that. But it was also how she truly felt. And her pouting about it would only ruin the mood and cast a shadow over the wedding and any of the remaining planning they had to do. Not to mention how awkward it would make things if Tripp did agree to allow Ari's studio to film their next project here on his ranch.

She wouldn't do that to Ari and Xavier. Which meant she needed to get it together and be okay with the fact that whatever happened between her and Tripp during her stay here was a one-off best forgotten the moment she boarded that plane for home.

There was a knock at her door. Dee straightened her spine and regretted the fact that she hadn't packed any lingerie. She was wearing an old nightshirt that read Do Not Disturb.

"Come in," she said.

Tripp opened the door, and even in the limited light from the hallway, the man was more handsome than ever. "Hey."

"Hey." Dee clenched her thighs together, slightly embarrassed by how much she wanted this man right now. She folded her arms over her chest, trying to hide the Pavlovian beading of her nipples in response to the gruff, sexy tenor of Tripp's voice. "Your sister and her family... They're really nice. You're lucky they live right next door."

"Yeah, I guess I am." Tripp shoved his hands in his pockets and made his way to the center of the room. "They really like you, too, by the way."

"I'm glad." Dee held her ground, resisting the urge to walk closer. "It was a fun night. I haven't played Taboo in ages."

"My sister loves that game." Tripp was making his way closer. "She plays it every chance she gets. She knows they have the advantage because they've known each other since the beginning of time."

"I can be pretty competitive," Dionna said, looking up at Tripp who now stood in front of her. "The fact that they have that kind of history is the only reason I didn't feel quite so bad about them kicking our ass in that game. But we made up for it when we took it to them in—"

Before she could finish, Tripp had looped his arms around her waist and covered her mouth with his. The kiss had taken her by surprise, but her eyes drifted closed and her hands clutched at the back of his black T-shirt.

His tongue teased the seam of her lips, and she willingly parted them, eager for another taste of his mouth. Tripp's hands glided down her back and over her bottom. This time he lifted her onto the desk as he continued their kiss.

Dee's hands drifted beneath the black fabric, her hands gliding up his back as she pressed her fingertips to his skin, pulling him toward her. Did he have any idea how desperate she was for his touch? How much she needed to feel him inside of her again?

Tripp yanked up the hem of her nightshirt, and she lifted her arms to allow him to tug it over her head. He dropped the fabric onto the floor and stood still a moment, as if mesmerized by the sight of her topless, seated on what was once his sister's desk.

"God, Dee, you are so fucking beautiful." His words sounded almost reverent as he grazed her bare skin with the back of his hand.

Her entire body warmed, and her pulse raced. Dee tried not to squirm as Tripp kissed his way across her chest and up the other shoulder. She cleared her throat and tried to regain her focus. "I think we should talk."

Tripp froze for a moment. She could feel his back stiffen beneath her fingertips. "Okay. So let's talk."

"I… I… Um… I realize that you're… That you don't…" She was babbling like an idiot. With every fluttery, sensual kiss Tripp pressed to her bare skin, the harder it became to think. To breathe. Yet, she wanted more. But first, she needed to ensure there wouldn't be any hard feelings on either side.

Dionna swallowed hard and tried again. "I know you don't do serious relationships, Tripp." He stopped kissing her neck, and his eyes met hers. "So I just wanted you to know I'm not expecting anything to come of this. In fact, I went into it knowing there wouldn't."

Tripp dropped his gaze momentarily, and she could swear she saw him frown. Finally, he met her gaze again. "And you'd be okay with that? With this being just a vacation fling?"

Now she winced. Because it hurt her to think that this was just sex for Tripp when for her it felt like the beginning of so much more. Still, she nodded.

"Of course." Dee forced a quiet laugh, despite the deep ache in her chest. "You live in Royal. I live in LA. What else would this possibly be?"

Tripp pulled back a moment and stared at her, his expression unreadable. "That's good to know," he said finally. "And since the clock is ticking on this thing, I think we should make the most of every day that we have left together, don't you?"

"Yes," she practically whispered the word. She could feel her eyebrows furrowing even as she forced a smile. "I guess we should."

There was something devilish in Tripp's smirk and in the flare of his nostrils. But when he dropped to his knees on the carpeted floor, she didn't have time to consider what was behind his expression.

"What are you—"

Before she could finish the question, Tripp had his large hands on her waist, gliding her panties down her hips and onto the floor. He set her on the edge of the desk, and before she could react, his mouth was on her, his tongue lashing at her already sensitive flesh.

Dee leaned back, her hands gripping the back of the desk, involuntary whimpers escaping her mouth as he licked and sucked her with increasing intensity. And the way he stared at her, practically daring her to look away. Her entire body trembled with an intensifying pleasure that felt overwhelming and yet like not enough all at the same time.

Her legs dangled awkwardly, and she tried to hold them open, giving his broad shoulders space. But then Tripp placed one leg and then the other over his shoulders. His smirk deepened as he dived two fingers inside of her and curved them.

"Tripp, oh my God!" she'd practically shouted in response to the incredible sensation of his fingers moving inside her and his mouth on her clit. Dee's belly tensed, her back arched and her head lolled back. Her biceps ached and trembled with the additional effort required just to stay upright. "Oh my God, yes. Yes, yes, yes."

Dee panted, her heart racing, as she shattered into pieces. Her inner walls pulsed, gripping his fingers.

Tripp pressed a kiss to her sex. Then down her inner thigh. Behind her knee. He watched with satisfaction as her chest heaved and she slowly came down from the intense high he'd given her.

He let her legs down and slowly rose to his bare feet—something she'd never found sexy on a man before. Tripp dragged the back of his hand across his lips and chin, gleaming with evidence of her pleasure. He flashed her the most wickedly delicious half smile. The kind of smile that indicated this was only the beginning of what he had in store for her.

Dionna swallowed hard, her chest still heaving. Her skin felt warm all over.

Tripp leaned in, his whiskered chin grazing her

shoulder as his lips brushed her ear. "You taste so fucking good."

How exactly did one respond to such a compliment?

She wanted to make a joke about it being the peach sangria sugar body scrub she'd just used in the shower. But the shiver that rippled down her spine impeded her ability to be quirky or clever.

"Turn around." Tripp's voice had deepened. Its lower register apparently also reaching down deep in her soul and strumming the parts of her body his clever mouth had just brought to orgasm.

"Wh-what?" Dee felt like she was in a haze, her mind too foggy to even comprehend basic instructions.

Tripp didn't repeat himself. Instead, he tugged her to her feet and turned her around, pressing her palms to the desk.

"Seriously, I'm all for fun and games. But if you're thinking of doing a strip search... I'm out." She'd finally found her voice and at least a hint of her ability to be a smart-ass. A natural reaction whenever she felt nervous.

And this Tripp—the infinitely sexy man who growled orders into her ear and glared at her with the intensity of a lion who hadn't eaten meat in a month—made her incredibly nervous.

Tripp chuckled, the low sound vibrating through her back, pressed to his stomach. He tweaked a beaded nipple as he leaned over and kissed her neck. "You got jokes. Cute."

Dionna could hear the crinkle of the foil packet

as he tore it open and the sound of his zipper as he tugged it down and sheathed himself. Tripp pressed one hand to her hip and the other pressed to her back as he bent her over the desk. Then both his hands were gone for a moment, just before he pressed himself inside her in a motion so quick that it took her by surprise, despite the fact that she'd been anticipating it. Craving it even.

"Oh my God," she muttered at the delicious sensation of being filled by Tripp. Seriously, why did he feel even bigger than he had just a few hours before? She couldn't help her soft whimper—her cheek pressed to her spiral planner on the desk.

She didn't care. If she had marks on her skin from the items on the desk, it would be well worth every moment of pleasure this man was giving her. And she wanted to give him the same. When she tensed her inner muscles, Tripp responded with a low growl of his own.

He took a deep breath and retreated, leaving just the head inside of her. He leaned over and whispered, "I wouldn't do that just yet, sweetheart. Not if you want this to last."

She did. In fact, a part of Dee wanted this moment to last forever. Another part of her wondered just how much more she could take.

"Please," she whimpered, a little angry with herself for begging for it. For him.

"Please what?" Tripp trailed a finger down one bare ass cheek.

"Fuck me. Please. Now."

She'd never said those words to anyone before. But even without him saying it expressly, she already knew that was exactly what he wanted to hear.

Dionna could hear the smirk in Tripp's voice.

"As you wish."

The glide felt so delicious as he pressed inside of her. Like a desperate itch that she couldn't reach, and someone had finally scratched. She pressed her lips together, determined not to moan, whimper or otherwise embarrass herself because the sensation of Tripp inside her felt better than words could say.

And as he started his continuous motion, his hand pressed to her low back, her murmurs grew louder. After a while, she didn't care. She just wanted more of him as she pressed her hips back to meet his thrusts.

Then Tripp lifted her leg, pressing her knee onto the desk. The hand that was on her hip glided down her stomach and flicked her clit, already sensitive and aching for more of his touch. Her pleasure spiraled, her head feeling lighter, until he drove her over the edge, his name on her lips until her throat felt hoarse.

Tripp groaned, the sound deeper than before, as the pulsing of her sex seemed to pull him over the edge, too. He leaned on his hands, now pressed to the desk on either side of her as they both tried to catch their breath. Finally, he dropped a soft kiss on her shoulder blade and patted her hip.

"Let me take care of this and I'll be right back."

Dee nodded, not capable of coherent speech. Once the bathroom door closed and she could hear the water running in the sink, she took a few more breaths before finally hoisting herself upright again, though she still leaned most of her weight on the desk. Her legs felt like noodles.

She sighed, glancing over at the bed, which felt like it was miles away. Well, at least if she tumbled to the floor, unable to make it across the room on what felt like newborn giraffe legs, the floor was covered in a thick plush carpeting that felt like heaven beneath her feet.

Dionna retrieved the silky pink underwear Tripp had discarded earlier. Then instead of grabbing her nightshirt, which she couldn't seem to find, she tugged the black T-shirt that smelled of citrus and sandalwood—just like Tripp—over her head. She didn't even care that it was inside out. Then she climbed into the bed and drifted off to sleep.

Tripp washed his hands, then dragged his fingers through his hair. His jaw and shoulders still tense. He stared at his reflection in the mirror, unsure who he was more upset with—Dee or himself.

He was pissed at himself because after more than a decade of living his best, relationship-free life, he'd finally met someone who made him reconsider the position. Made him want to step out of his safety zone. He was agitated with Dee because before he could share his revelation with her, she'd declared that she wasn't interested.

Tripp scratched at his chin—overdue for a shave—and glared at his reflection. Had he really been that off about Dee? About what she wanted?

Then again, maybe his sister was right. Maybe the only reason he'd even considered a relationship with Dee was because it felt impossible. So maybe it wasn't really what he wanted either.

Tripp heaved a sigh and slipped off his unzipped jeans, setting them on top of the clothes hamper. He'd deal with all of the confusing thoughts running through his head like a herd of cattle in search of water tomorrow. Right now, he just wanted to sleep.

He stepped out of the bathroom in his boxer briefs and bare feet, in search of the T-shirt he'd shed earlier. It was no longer on the floor. When he glanced over at the bed, Dee was cuddled under the comforter, a hint of his black T-shirt peeking above it.

His frown softened. There was something sweet and tender about the fact that she'd donned his T-shirt before crawling into bed. As he walked closer, Dee was breathing softly and down for the count. Tripp chuckled to himself and made a mental note to tease her the next day about how he'd laid her ass to sleep.

He stood beside the bed for a moment. Dee was already asleep, so he could return to his own bed. After all, it's what he would normally do. But he couldn't resist the surprising desire to crawl into bed with Dee. To wake up to her the following morning.

Tripp turned off the desk light, then slipped beneath the covers. Dee, who was lying on her side, facing away from him, scooted back against him. Tripp turned over onto his side and wrapped his arm around her stomach, tugging her closer, so he was the big spoon to her little spoon. He pressed his nose to her hair, inhaling the delicious scent of coconut and vanilla.

"Thought you were asleep." He pressed a kiss to her ear.

"I'm a light sleeper." Her face was still buried in the pillow. "I thought you would leave."

"It's my house. It'd be kind of weird if I left." He couldn't help fucking with her.

She elbowed him in the side, and he laughed. Dionna turned in his arms so she was facing him. She gently cradled his cheek. "That's not what I meant, and you know it. I figured you would go back to your own room." She searched his eyes in the mostly dark room, lit only by a sliver of moonlight coming through the sheer curtains that shielded the balcony doors. Dee dragged her thumb across his lower lip. "Didn't take you for a cuddler."

"I'm not usually." Tripp shrugged, liking the feel of Dionna's soft hands on his rough skin. "Why? Would you like me to leave?"

"No. Don't go." Her response was instant, without a moment's hesitation. She pressed a kiss to his lips. "I like having you here."

It felt as though Dee's words had reached into his chest and squeezed his heart. He swallowed roughly and nodded. "I like having you here, too."

Her eyes glinted as she smiled, caressing his cheek.

Tripp pressed a kiss to her palm. "Good night, Dionna."

"Good night, Tripp." She turned over, wiggling so her ass was snuggled against him. Then she laid her arm on top of his arm, draped over her waist. A few moments later, Dee had fallen back to sleep again.

There was nothing Tripp wanted more than to join her in la-la land. But instead, he lay awake racking his brain for the answer to Dee's earlier question.

You live in Royal. I live in LA. What else would this possibly be?

Because despite what either of them had said, he couldn't help feeling that whatever was going on between him and Dionna was meant to be much more than a fling.

Twelve

Dionna stood in the horse stable at The Noble Spur and stroked the silky black mane of Deuce, the majestic Arabian horse she'd been riding the past few days.

Dee had reluctantly agreed to go horseback riding with Tripp the day after they'd first slept together. She'd been terrified, but Tripp had been so patient and encouraging. And Deuce seemed to sense her fear. Yet, he'd been gentle and docile. She'd fallen in love with riding.

Tripp had made time to take Dionna riding every afternoon since she loved it so much. She adored the time they spent together riding on the Nobles' vast property. In fact, she loved every single minute she got to spend with Tripp.

The passionate nights they'd spent together. Falling asleep in each other's arms after sharing stories about their lives and their families. Starting each day together making and eating breakfast. Planning Ari and Ex's prewedding festivities over lunch. Exploring the ranch on horseback in the afternoons. Then venturing into Royal each evening after he'd finished his day on the ranch and she'd finished hers working remotely.

Last evening, they'd taken a mosaic class together at the antique shop in town called Priceless, housed in a big red barn. It was another activity Dee hadn't thought she'd enjoy, but it'd been fun. More so because they'd done it together.

Since the night they'd first made love, Tripp had spent every night in her bed or she in his. But she hadn't gotten around to asking Tripp about filming on his land. Or about the other idea she had that he would probably consider even crazier.

Dee sighed heavily, thinking of the call she'd had earlier with Molly. Marcus was waiting on an answer, and he wasn't known for being a patient man. She'd already run the idea past Ari, and she'd loved it. Now she just needed to get up the nerve to ask Tripp.

She nuzzled Deuce's snout, then handed the gentle yet majestic animal a well-deserved apple. She patted his head. "You're such a sweet boy."

"I'm glad you two are getting along so well." Tripp grinned as he led his reddish-brown quarter horse, Nick Fury, to his stall and closed the gate.

Tripp tossed Nick an apple, then glanced around to ensure no one else was around. He slipped his arms around her waist and gave her a kiss that made her skin warm and her pulse race. Tripp leaned his forehead against hers. "Is it weird that I'm suddenly a little jealous of my horse?"

"Trust me, I'd prefer to be riding you." Dee cradled his whiskered cheek and kissed him again.

Reluctantly, she pulled out of his arms. Partly because she didn't want one of the ranch hands to catch them making out in the barn—which had come close to happening twice before. But also because she needed to put on her business hat. Something that would be hard to do when she was cradled against Tripp's solid chest and other hard parts.

"Tripp, there's something I need to talk to you about."

"Okay." His expression became more serious. He shoved his hands in his pockets. "Does Ari not like the plans we've come up with so far?" He shifted his hat enough to wipe sweat from his forehead with the back of his sleeve.

"Ari will probably end up revamping the reception menu. But that's not what I want to talk to you about. This isn't related to the wedding. It's a business proposal."

"All right." Tripp's face took on that unreadable expression again.

"I... Uh... That Western about the Black cowboy we're filming... Well, we're trying to land Marcus Maybury for the lead role, and we're this close to signing him, but we've run into a small problem."

Tripp folded his arms, his legs planted wide. "Let me guess, he wants more money."

"They always want more money." Dee waved a hand. "That I can handle. It's just that Marcus believes this story could possibly put us in the running for Cannes and some of the other big film festivals. Ari and I believe that, too. Which means, this could be the breakout role Marcus has been waiting on, and the breakout film that would launch this studio to the next level."

"But…" He eyed her cautiously.

"But Marcus is a method actor and he is all about authenticity. So he won't accept the role if we film at a studio in Cali. To come on board, he's insisting that we actually film the movie in Texas, where the story is set." Dee kept her voice steady, despite the sound of her heart pounding in her ears.

"Good for him." Tripp nodded, seemingly impressed. "Enough with all of these sad green screen films."

"Which brings me to my proposal." Dionna stood taller, her shoulders back as her eyes met his. "That unused land you all have been deciding what to do with… What if we filmed the movie there?" She forced a big smile and held her breath.

"You want to film *here*?" Tripp asked incredulously. "On The Noble Spur?"

"Yes. And like I said, this is a business proposal—not a favor. So we'd pay you for the use of your land."

"Hmm…" Tripp rubbed his chin thoughtfully, his gaze elsewhere. "That would mean the place would

be overrun with your film crew and you'd be filming at all hours of the day." He seemed to be talking
more to himself than to her.

"We're not a major studio, so we operate with no
more crew than is necessary to get the job done," she
assured him. "As for the hours, since Ari is an actor,
too, she's sensitive to keeping the cast and crew on
set too long. Besides, the area of land we're talking
about is quite a distance from your place. So filming
shouldn't disrupt business here on the ranch."

"Dee, I need you to lose the bright, shiny, happy
sales pitch for a minute and just talk to me. Not like
I'm some random vendor." Tripp leveled his gaze with
hers. He stepped closer and lowered his voice. "Talk
to me like I'm the man who knows how every inch
of your skin tastes. The man whose name you call
until your voice goes hoarse."

Dee sank her teeth into her lower lip, her skin rag-
ing with fire and the space between her thighs damp
and wanting. She nodded. "Okay."

"Is this going to turn into a shit show? Create a
circus that'll piss off all my neighbors? Will there be
any damage to the land or danger to my animals?"
he asked.

"No, of course not." Dionna placed a gentle hand
on his arm. "I know how much you love this ranch
and this town. I'd never do anything to jeopardize
either of them."

"Then why the whole sales shtick?" Tripp raised
a brow.

"Because I didn't want to make it seem like I was

using our *relationship* to pressure you to agree to this." Dionna leaned into him, her hands pressed to his chest as she gazed up at him. "I'd love to film here, but only if that's something you'd want, too."

Tripp sucked in a deep breath and nodded. "All right."

"As in all right, you'll do it?"

"As in all right, I'm considering it. As long as we can come to terms on a price."

"Of course. Thank you, Tripp." She resisted the desire to squeal with joy. "But there is one more thing I need to ask."

His raised eyebrow made it clear that she was pushing it. But she asked anyway.

"In the spirit of authenticity, Marcus also insists that we have a consultant on the set. You know, someone who will ensure that everything we're doing is accurate and credible. Someone like...*you*."

"Me?" Tripp jabbed a thumb to his chest and took a step back. "C'mon, Dee, you can't be serious. I'm a rancher. Not a Hollywood movie consultant."

"We don't need you to be Hollywood. In fact, that's the very opposite of what we need you to be." She grabbed his hand as he started to pull away. "All we need is for you to be your charming, knowledgeable, well-connected self. Nothing more, nothing less."

"It would take time away from my work here on the ranch."

"I know. But the fee will cover hiring a few new ranch hands and maybe promoting someone like Roy to take on a bigger role. And you still have Tess to help with the office stuff. She was just saying the other night that she was ready to take on a bigger role with the ranch again now that they have a nanny." Dionna tried not to sound too eager. "Besides, you said that you love the ranch, but a part of you wanted to do something else. Maybe this is that something. You could make a career out of this."

"I have a career." He glanced around the barn, then rubbed his chin. "But maybe it could be a fun side hustle."

"Even better." Dee smiled. "But I need to know as soon as possible. And I know you said your mom wanted to be an actress. So if it'll sweeten the pot, I'm sure we could get your parents in the film as extras. It might not be a speaking role, but it'd definitely give them bragging rights."

"That means we'd see a lot more of each other, right?"

Dee nodded, her belly fluttering.

"All right. We can move forward on one condition." Tripp slipped her arm through his, and they headed back toward the house.

"Name it." Dee tried to stay focused on the issue at hand rather than the warmth and electricity that crawled down her spine in response to his touch and being so close to him.

"Seems to me you would need to stay another week or so to give us time to sort out the contract, decide on exactly where we should film, maybe where to source supplies… Things like that."

Dee could barely contain her grin. "Funny. Ari

mentioned the same thing this morning. I have meetings in LA and New York coming up. But Ari suggested that for now—just while we work all of this out—maybe I could make Royal my home base. If that's okay with—"

Tripp pulled her into his arms and kissed her, setting her entire body on fire and making her wish they were inside the house and away from prying eyes right now.

Dee finally forced herself to pull free. She glanced around, hoping they hadn't given one of the ranch hands—or worse, his sister, Tess—an unexpected peep show.

"I take that as a *yes*." Dee smiled.

"You can take that as a *hell yes*." Tripp leaned in to kiss her again.

She gave his shoulder a gentle shove. "Calm down, tiger. Someone, like your sister, might see us."

He dropped a quick kiss on her lips anyway. "I don't care."

Dionna sucked in a deep breath, her smile waning because she did care. She felt slightly irritated that Tripp was suddenly trying to change their agreement and a hint of guilt because she still wanted to keep their relationship a secret.

Yes, this arrangement would extend their little liaison. She was as grateful for that as he was. But it didn't change the fact that Tripp's life was here in Royal and hers was in LA. At some point, they'd have to come to terms with that hard, cold reality and this relationship would be doomed.

"I care." Her voice was soft, steeped with apology. "We both know what this is… What it has to be." Dee touched his cheek, her heart breaking at the disappointment she saw behind his eyes. "So there's no point in worrying Xavier and getting Ari's hopes up unnecessarily. If your decision is predicated on…"

"It isn't," Tripp sighed, then offered her a cursory smile. He extended a hand. "As long as we can come to terms, we have a deal."

"Really?" Forgetting herself for a moment, Dionna jumped into his arms and hugged him.

Tripp laughed when she stepped back and cleared her throat, glancing around again.

"Thank you, Tripp. I promise to do everything in my power to ensure that this is the best possible experience for you," Dee said.

Tripp cradled her cheek. His warm gaze reflected a deep affection that made her belly flutter. "Trust me, sweetheart, it already is."

Thirteen

Tripp stepped out of the shower, dried himself off and wrapped a towel around his waist. He wiped the condensation from the bathroom mirror, pulled out his razor and carefully trimmed his beard.

It still felt odd that Ari's company wanted to film on his land and asked him to serve as a consultant on the film. The first request didn't bother him as long as the film crew didn't damage his property, disrupt his business or piss off his neighbors. The second request had given him pause.

Yes, he knew ranch life inside and out. And he was well versed on the history of Black cowboys in Texas and in other parts of the country. Both his parents and grandparents had ensured that he and his sister knew their history and never, *ever* forgot it.

They didn't have the luxury of pretending the past hadn't happened just because it was unpleasant. He knew all too well that atrocities forgotten were destined to be repeated.

Still, being a Black rancher in the present didn't necessarily make him the best person to consult on a film about Black cowboys in the past. But he'd read the script. Ari and Dionna and that pretty boy actor, Marcus Maybury, were right. This was an important story. One that deserved to be told authentically rather than being swept under the rug—where so much of the history of Black cowboys in this country had been relegated.

Maybe he'd initially agreed to sign on to the project as a way to keep Dionna here—in Royal, in his home and in his bed. But it was about more than that now. He believed in the project. So he'd do whatever he could to ensure the story was told authentically. Still, he was glad Dee had promised to support him in this new role in any way she could. Her promise had been comforting. Much like the woman herself.

Tripp rinsed the razor and put it away. He leaned against the doorframe, watching Dionna asleep in his bed. His mouth curved in an involuntary smile. Something he'd been doing often since Dionna had come into his life.

Not that he wasn't happy before. But since he and Dee had connected, his life felt...*different*. Being with Dee brought him a surprising sense of contentment. As much as he loved being with Dionna physically, he'd been just as content in the quiet moments they shared. Settling on the sofa to watch a movie they'd both seen before. Playing a hand of gin rummy. Or riding Deuce and Nick Fury on one of The Noble Spur's trails. And he loved that Dee seemed to truly enjoy spending time with his sister and her family. That despite being an LA girl her entire life, she fit into his life here in Royal so well.

Tripp sighed quietly, then made his way to his closet to get dressed. A few more minutes, then he'd wake Dee.

Keely Tucker, who was creating Ariana's bridal gown, had arrived in town. Tripp had promised Ex and Ariana that he'd help Keely source her materials and accessories in Royal, keeping with the bride and groom's determination to work with local vendors. There was a mixer at the Texas Cattleman's Club that evening. It was the perfect way to introduce Keely to as many vendors as possible in a single night. But he'd much prefer to spend the evening at home with Dionna.

They'd had an early dinner, made love, and had both fallen asleep. They would probably have slept through the night if he hadn't obligated himself to attend the mixer tonight. He'd keep his word, show up to the event and connect Keely with local shop owners. But once he fulfilled his obligation, he'd be right back at The Noble Spur, lying beside Dee.

Tripp treasured every moment he and Dionna got to spend together. Perhaps because they were on borrowed time. Soon Dee would pack her bags and return to LA for good. Whenever he thought of her leaving, a knot tightened in his gut.

He didn't want Dee to go, and he couldn't help thinking that she didn't want to leave either. Not just because of him. Dionna seemed happier and more relaxed in Royal. As if a burdensome weight had been lifted from her shoulders.

Tripp sat on the edge of his bed and traced a finger down Dee's arm a few times until she gradually awakened. Her dark brown eyes fluttered open.

"Hey." Her bashful smile did something to him. *Every. Damn. Time.*

"Hey, sweetheart." He threaded their fingers and kissed the back of her hand. "I hated to wake you, but the event kicks off in about an hour. I know you hate having to rush."

Dee stretched and yawned, wiping the sleep from her eyes. She'd spent the past few days flying all over the country. Dee had flown to meetings in LA and Chicago. She'd flown to New York to meet with Marcus Maybury, who was officially on board for the film. Then she'd returned to Royal earlier that day. It was no wonder she'd fallen asleep the moment her head had finally hit the pillow.

"What time is it?" she asked through a yawn.

"Quarter to seven, and the party kicks off at eight."

Dee released his hand and buried her face in the pillow. "I need at least another hour of sleep to feel human. You go ahead to the party. If I'm up to it, I'll join you later."

"Of course. I understand how exhausted you must

be." Tripp tried not to sound disappointed. "I'm only going myself to make sure Keely connects with the vendors she'll need to work with."

"Oh gosh!" Dee sat up. "I completely forgot. I'll hop in the shower and get dressed."

"No, get some sleep, babe." He braced her hip, holding her in place. "I've got this. If you're up for it later, give me a call and I'll come back for you. If not, no problem. Stay in bed, get some sleep, and I'll be back as soon as I can. All right?"

"You're sure you don't mind?" Dee kissed him, then cradled his jaw.

"I'll be fine." Tripp stroked her cheek. "Now go back to sleep. I'll see you in a bit."

He grabbed his shoes and jacket, turned off the light and closed the door behind him. He hadn't left the house and already he was counting the moments until he'd be holding Dee in his arms again.

Dionna had slept another hour, then got up, showered and got dressed. It seemed silly to ask Tripp to come back to pick her up. So she used her rideshare app to request a ride to the Texas Cattleman's Club instead. She entered the club, as a friend of Tripp's, then made her way to the bar, hoping that the bartender could make a decent mojito.

She sipped her drink and sighed with contentment. Then she dropped a generous tip in the glass jar on the counter. Dionna perched on a stool with her back to the bar as she studied the room. Eventually, she'd find Tripp. But for now, sit there and take the temperature of the room before she ventured into the crowd.

Dee had enjoyed every experience in Royal. Meeting locals. Going out to eat. But this was the biggest event she'd attended there thus far. And she was always more comfortable taking a big event like this slow. Hanging out on the edges like a wallflower until she got comfortable enough to wade into the crowd of unfamiliar faces with its requisite small talk with strangers and mindless chitchat.

She wasn't antisocial. She was just very introverted. She liked people as much as the next person. But she needed quiet time before and after such an outing to recharge her batteries. Otherwise, she'd be cranky and completely drained.

"Milan!"

Dionna's head snapped toward the sound of the voice for two reasons. First, because she hadn't gotten a chance to meet Milan in person yet, though Ari had already booked her as the makeup artist for the wedding. Second, because she recognized the voice that had called her.

It was Tripp's.

Dee took another sip from her glass as she watched Tripp open his arms to a gorgeous Afro-Latina woman whose hair was light brown with blond streaks running through it and with flawless makeup.

The woman kissed his cheek, and they shared an intimate embrace that fired up heat in Dee's cheeks and gave her a sense of unease.

Tripp was friendly and harmlessly flirtatious. She

realized that. And despite the time they'd spent together, she certainly had no claim on him. Still, she couldn't help the knot tightening in her gut and the ache in her chest. The gaze between them as he continued to hold her hand felt much more intimate than a friendship.

Two women perched on the empty barstools beside her and ordered their drinks. The blonde elbowed her friend—a redhead—in the side and nodded across the room.

"Looks like things are heating up again between Tripp Noble and his ex," the blonde said, as if it was the most delicious piece of gossip.

"Which one?" the redhead asked with a bitter laugh.

"Milan Valez, the makeup artist from PURE. They're right over there." The blonde pointed impatiently.

"Ahh…" The redhead sipped the cosmo the bartender handed her. "I was so sure she was the one who would finally get our eternal bachelor to settle down."

"So did she." The blonde chuckled, then muttered, "Welcome to the club, honey."

"Amen." The two women clinked their glasses together and giggled. "Now c'mon. This is a mixer, so we should be mixing it up. Grab your drink and let's go. Got my sights set on a handsome rancher at two o'clock."

The women laughed and then they were gone.

Dee sucked in a deep breath. Her face was hot

and her eyes stung with tears, and she wasn't even sure why.

She and Tripp had never talked about being exclusive. In fact, she was the one who'd been adamant about keeping their relationship a secret. So what right did she have to be jealous, even if Milan Valez was his ex?

That was what the logical part of her brain insisted. But her heart felt...betrayed.

Dee glanced over to where Tripp and Milan were still engaged in an intimate conversation. He leaned down closer to the woman who was at least a head shorter than him. Presumably to be heard over the din of music and conversation. Yet, she couldn't help thinking of all the times he'd leaned in like that to whisper something intimate and adorable to her. Or to nuzzle her neck.

I was so sure she was the one who would finally get our eternal bachelor to settle down.

So did she. Welcome to the club, honey.

The women's derisive words and laughter rang in her ears.

Dee's neck and cheeks burned. She wasn't sure who she felt sorrier for—Milan, who'd evidently believed that what was happening between her and Tripp was real or herself. Because despite what she'd been telling herself, there was apparently a small part of her that had been holding on to that same hope.

Dionna jumped down from the stool, inadvertently tipping over her half-full mojito glass. "I'm such a klutz. I'm so sorry."

"Happens all the time." The tall handsome bartender retrieved her glass and mopped up the mess before she could grab a handful of napkins to do it herself. The man leaned in and lowered his voice. "Don't let the sour grapes get to you." He winked. "I'll get you another drink."

"No, you don't have to—" Dee raised a hand to object, but he was already gone. She didn't want another drink. All she wanted was to call a rideshare and get the hell out of there. Pretend she'd never even been there. Then retreat to her room and claim a headache or the flu. Maybe mono.

"Dionna, I thought that was you." A big smile spread across Tessa's face as she and Ryan approached the bar hand in hand.

God, the two of them were beyond adorable. And Tess had been so sweet to her. She wouldn't just bolt on Tripp's sister. No matter how badly she wanted to get out of there.

"Hey, Tess, Ryan. How are you?" Dionna flashed her widest smile as she accepted hugs from the couple. "You two look great."

"So do you." Tess held her at arm's length and studied her Mediterranean blue Kay Unger jumpsuit with the overlay skirt over midnight blue crepe pants and nude heels. "This jumpsuit is absolutely gorgeous."

Dee thanked Tess and flashed her an awkward smile. She accepted her drink from the bartender and dropped another tip in his jar. The guy was working overtime to keep her afloat tonight.

When she'd gotten dressed in this outfit earlier, all she could think of was what Tripp would think of it and how long it would take him to get her out of it. Now the memory made her want to start bawling like an infant who'd been served spinach when what she'd wanted was sweet potatoes.

"Dee, honey, are you okay?" Tessa looked concerned.

Ryan took the hint, said he was going over to say hello to someone, kissed his wife's cheek and promised to catch up with them later.

"Yes. Sure. Of course," Dee babbled, her smile feeling strange and plastic. She'd never been good at faking her feelings. Whatever was in her head and her heart was automatically plastered over her face. "I just got here actually. And I'm not really feeling so well."

"I'm so sorry to hear that, sweetie. Where's Tripp?" Tessa's gaze swept the place. "If he can't take you home, I will."

Home.

Dee hadn't really thought about it before, but so many times Tripp had said "Let's go home" or "When we get back home" to her. As if his home was her home, too. But it wasn't. She was an interloper staying on his family's estate. Any thoughts of The Noble Spur being her home was an indulgence in a schoolgirl fantasy that would never, *ever* come true.

And dammit. Now Tess was blurry as Dee's eyes clouded with tears. Had her new friend noticed?

"That isn't necessary, really. I took a car service

here tonight. Tripp doesn't even know I'm here. There's no need to bother him with—"

"Is that why you're so upset?" There was a mixture of pity and fury in Tessa's voice as she stared at her brother standing across the room. Tripp's hand rested low on Milan's back, and he seemed to be introducing her to Ariana's stylist Keely Tucker, who'd been engaged to create Ari's custom bridal gown.

"No, of course not. Why would I be upset about that?" Dee could feel her face shifting into a frown, even as she attempted to ratchet up her unnatural smile.

God, I must look like some bizarre serial killer right now.

"Sweetie, I know what you both are saying, but I can see what's really going on with you two." Tessa's words felt more like a warm hug than chastisement. "I realize as Tripp's sister my words might not mean very much to you right now, but I'm confident this isn't what you think this is."

It felt like a load of bricks were piled on Dee's chest and she could barely breathe. "I should go. It was good seeing you again, Tess. Have a great time tonight."

Dionna hugged Tess, chugged the last of her drink and made her way toward the coat check to claim her coat. She headed outside, not caring that she hadn't called the rideshare service yet and there might not even be one available on this chilly March night.

She'd walk all the way back to The Noble Spur in her four-inch heels if she had to.

Dee sniffled as the cold air assaulted her nostrils and wetness stained her cheeks. She pulled the coat around her tightly and dug her phone out of her coat pocket.

"Dionna!"

Dee didn't answer. Instead, she cringed and turned her back to the source of the sound as she quickly dabbed at her damp eyes and wet cheeks with her knuckle.

"Dee, what's going on? What are you doing out here? It's freezing tonight." Tripp stood in front of her without a coat, his arms folded over his chest as he shivered.

"Nothing's wrong. I just…" She gazed at the darkened fields just over his shoulder. "I shouldn't have come. I'd like to go back ho—" She stopped herself. "I'd like to go back to the ranch. I think I'm just going to go to my room and crash for the night. Maybe even for the weekend."

Tripp lifted her chin, forcing her gaze to meet his. "You've been crying."

It wasn't a question, so she didn't bother denying it.

She pulled out of his grip and sniffled again, wrapping her arms around herself. "Like you said, it's cold out. I think I'm coming down with something."

"You were supposed to call me. I would've come for you."

"Is that so you'd have a heads-up before I showed up and surprised you while you were flirting with half the women in the room?" Dee squeezed her eyes shut, hating herself for saying exactly what she was thinking.

"What are you talking about?" Tripp grasped her shoulders. "You're the one who's insisting that we keep this a secret. I wanted to tell Ari and Ex. Hell, I would've told anyone who wanted to listen by now. I've kept my mouth shut because it's what *you* wanted." His jaw clenched and his eyes flashed in the darkness. "So what the hell has gotten into you tonight? Tess said you looked upset. Is this about me talking to Milan and Keely? I never took you for the jealous type, Dee."

She hated that he sounded monumentally disappointed in her when it was her who had every right to be disappointed in him.

"You never mentioned that Milan Valez was more than just the makeup artist who made over your sister for the bachelor auction. And you certainly never mentioned that she was your freaking ex," she whispered loudly, pointing an accusatory finger at him.

Tripp sucked in a deep breath and released it, visible in the night air. "I didn't," he acknowledged. "At the time, you and I weren't involved. It was strictly a business decision. So I made the conscious decision *not* to bring up our history because I didn't want her to be selected or dismissed based on our past connection. I wanted Ari to choose Milan based on her own merits because I know Mimi well enough to know that's what she would want."

So now it was *Mimi*?

"Okay, *Mimi* would've wanted to stand on her own two feet. I get it." She really did.

Dee hadn't ever used her friendship with Ari or her family to get a job in the past. An opportunity... Yes. But she'd wanted them to choose her because she was damn good at what she did. Not because of whose names were in her high school yearbook.

"But once we were..." Dionna glanced around the dark parking lot.

"Involved?" Tripp glared at her, his patience clearly wearing thin.

"Why didn't you mention your relationship with her then?" she asked.

Tripp toned down the self-righteous glare and sighed. He rubbed at his forehead. "I've already hurt her enough, even if it wasn't intentional. I couldn't let her lose out on a career-making opportunity because of me. I wouldn't have been able to forgive myself for that."

"So you didn't trust me enough to tell me the truth? Even though you were sleeping with me. Is that really what you take me for? Some vindictive woman who has it in for everyone her man has ever slept with in the past?"

"Like you didn't trust me enough to find out if there was anything actually happening between me and Milan? You just jumped to the conclusion that I'm some cheating dickhead who'd leave you home in bed and then come hook up with my ex?"

The hurt in his voice came across more loudly than the anger. She cringed, her chest uneasy with guilt.

Dee inhaled deeply and folded her arms. "If you'd seen things from my vantage point, you would've thought the same thing."

"No, I wouldn't have, Dee. Because I know you... Or at least, I thought I did. And I already know that the woman I adore would never do anything to hurt me intentionally. So I would've given you the benefit of the doubt."

Dee stood there, staring at him. What he'd said was sweet and warm, and it made her feel foolish. But hadn't her ex been good at saying all the right things and making her feel guilty when they both knew he was the culpable one?

Her mouth fell open, but she didn't know what to say. The chill in the air seeped through her bones. She shivered, wrapping her arms around herself.

Tripp sighed. And though she was wearing a coat and he was only wearing a blazer, he stripped it off and settled the jacket that smelled like him on her shoulders.

"If you want to go back to the ranch... Fine. I'll take you there myself. Just give me a minute. I'd promised to take Keely back to her hotel. I need to ask my friend Jay to see her home instead. Just, please step inside while you wait. It's freezing out here. You're gonna get sick." Tripp placed a hand on her back. The other gestured toward the club.

Dee nodded.

They took a few steps toward the door, but suddenly Tripp froze. He turned to her. "No, you need to come back inside. We won't stay, if you don't want

to. But Milan is looking forward to meeting you tonight because I couldn't shut up about you, and Keely
is looking forward to seeing a familiar face. So hate
me if you want to for absolutely fucking nothing.
That's fine. But the last thing either of us want is to
insult two of the key creatives Ariana is relying on
for her big day."

"Are you *telling me* I have to go back in there?" Dionna folded her arms and glared right back at Tripp.

"Fuck it," he whispered beneath his breath. "*Yes*,
Dionna Reed, I'm *telling* you that you need to stop
acting like a spoiled, immature, jealous brat. To come
inside and introduce yourself to these two *very* professional women who we *need* for this wedding. And,
yes, I expect you to behave like the classy professional woman you've always been. Now, whether you
choose to do it or not, that's up to you. But it seems
your only other alternative is to stand out here freezing your ass off while you're waiting for a rideshare
that may or may not come." He extended his elbow.
"So what's it going to be?"

Dee huffed, her breath fogging the air around her.
She slipped her arm through his and allowed him to
lead her back inside.

Tripp slipped his blazer back on and checked Dee's
coat again. Then he escorted her inside the main
space.

"There you two are. You must be Dionna." The
woman she recognized as Milan stood behind them
at the bar with Keely Tucker flanking her.

"Yes." Dee turned around and flashed the woman

a smile as bright as the morning sun and extended her hand. "And you must be…"

Before she could finish speaking, Milan had pulled Dee into a hug.

"Sorry." The woman finally released her. "I'm Milan Valez. Thanks to you both I'll be doing the makeup at the wedding of Ariana Ramos, whom I absolutely adore. I honestly can't thank you enough. I've always made a big deal about wanting to do this on my own and not needing help. I'm glad Tripp didn't listen to me this time."

The woman's excited grin lit up the entire room and melted Dionna's heart. She felt awful for assuming bad motives of this woman and of Tripp.

"It was your flawless work that got you this job, Milan." Dionna took the woman's hand in both of hers, her smile genuine this time. "Tripp just made sure Ari got to see what you were capable of. The rest was all you."

Milan's cheeks flushed and her eyes were shiny with tears of gratitude. She hugged Tripp, and then she hugged Dee again.

"You couldn't possibly know how much that means to me." Milan laughed, wiping at her eyes. "But thank you just the same. And thank you, Tripp, for introducing me to Keely. She's already recommended me for a few other high-profile events."

"That's fantastic," Dee and Tripp said simultaneously. They glanced at each other momentarily before returning their attention to Keely.

Dee exchanged hugs with Keely, Ariana's stylist and friend, whom it was always good to see.

"I hear you've been here in town working your magic, as always," Keely said.

"It's nothing, really. And I haven't done it alone. Tripp has been amazing. He's remarkably resourceful."

"True, but don't be so modest, Dionna." Milan waved a hand. "I've heard so much about you. You're a hit around town. And Tripp here hasn't been able to stop gushing about you all night."

Dee swallowed hard, her throat dry as she glanced over at Tripp. She felt like a complete ass for thinking the worst of him. He'd come here and done *exactly* what he'd promised to do. And he'd gone out of his way to make her look good, too.

He slipped his arm around her waist and smiled broadly. "Every word of it is true."

Tripp's words were kind and the gesture of pulling her closer was warm. But she could feel the tension in his arm, in his voice and in the heat radiating off of him. But he was too much of a gentleman to say all of the things he was probably thinking about her right now.

She'd screwed up. *Immensely.*

Dee wished she could take back the things she'd said. But it was too late. And things would never be the same.

Fourteen

Tripp climbed into his truck, clicked his seat belt and pulled out onto the street.

After their argument in the parking lot, he and Dee had stayed at the club another couple of hours. And while they'd been personable, friendly and full of smiles for everyone else, the tension still lingered between them.

He'd been glad when his sister told him Dionna was there at the club but stunned when she'd informed him that she seemed to be upset and that she was leaving. And he'd been more than a little pissed that Dee had essentially accused him of trying to hook up with his ex when the two of them were...

Tripp frowned and gripped the wheel tighter. To be honest, he wasn't quite sure what the two of them were.

Saying they were *lovers* felt ridiculous. Dee didn't want anyone else to know about them, so he certainly couldn't call her his girlfriend. And whatever the hell this was, it was certainly more than a hookup.

Tripp dragged a hand down his face and turned onto the road that led toward the ranch, glad his friend Jay Chatman had offered to take Keely back to her hotel. He and Dee had been able to keep up the pretense that nothing was wrong during the event. But the moment they'd exited the Texas Cattleman's Club, an uncomfortable silence descended over them. They'd been in the truck driving for at least five minutes and neither of them had said a word. He was about to speak when Dee turned to him suddenly.

"Tripp, I'm sorry I was so awful earlier. I'm not usually a jealous…ass." She sighed heavily and swept her twists over one shoulder. "I honestly don't know what came over me tonight. I had no right, nor did you give me any reason, to behave the way I did. I'm truly sorry."

Tripp could feel the heat of her stare as she waited for him to say something. Anything. But he wouldn't let her off that easy. Not after she'd thought him capable of casually leaving her in bed and then…what? Hooking up with someone else?

No, they hadn't ever talked about exclusivity. In fact, they hadn't really discussed the relationship at all beyond the fact that they needed to keep it under wraps. Her choice, not his. Still, he thought it was understood that he was with Dee and no one else.

"I didn't have the right to behave that way because you never committed to any obligation between us, and I never asked you to. You gave me no reason to be jealous because...because you were doing exactly what you'd promised you would. And the sweet things you said about me to Mimi and Keely... The way I behaved this evening... I don't deserve them..." Her words trailed off as he stared at the road ahead without reply. "You can stop me anytime," she added with a bitter laugh.

"I will." Tripp gripped the wheel tightly. "When I actually disagree with anything you've said."

"Ouch." Dee faced forward in her seat again and settled her hands on her lap. "I certainly deserved that, didn't I?"

"You certainly did," he said without hesitation. After a few moments of heavy silence, he said, "God, Dee, I am absolutely furious with you right now. I realize that we haven't known each other as long as you and Ari. But I guess I thought you knew me well enough to know I'm not the kind of guy who pulls this kind of juvenile shit. If I'd wanted to be with someone else, I would've been. I'm with you because I want to be with you and just you. And the only reason that isn't common knowledge around here is because keeping it a secret was what you wanted—"

"I know. You're right. And I do know you better than that, Tripp."

"Then what was that scene outside the club tonight

about? That wasn't you, Dee. At least, I didn't think it was. But hell, maybe I was wrong."

"No, you weren't. I honestly didn't even recognize myself tonight." Dee turned toward the window.

"Then what the hell happened tonight? You know why I was there."

"I know. But the moment I saw you with Milan and these two women sat down beside me and they were saying that it looked like you and your ex were getting back together…" She heaved a quiet sigh. "I lost it."

"Why?" He needed to know why she'd acted so out of character tonight.

"Seeing you two tonight took me back to what happened a year ago when I discovered that the man I was in love with was in love with someone else." Dee huffed quietly.

"And you had no idea?"

"Honestly? I'd been blind to all of the little signs that there was someone else because I didn't *want* it to be true. But my blind belief in him didn't make me some loyal, ride-or-die chick. It just made me naive and stupid. I promised myself I'd never, ever let someone gaslight me like that again."

Silence filled the cabin of the truck, neither of them speaking. He pulled into the long drive of The Noble Spur and parked his truck, then turned to her.

"I'm sorry about what your ex did to you, Dee. I really am." Tripp settled a hand on her arm. "But I'm *not* him. I would *never* treat you or anyone else that way. If it was over, I'd have the guts to tell you so.

Don't make me pay for his fuckup. Got enough of my own to make amends for."

"You're right. I'm sorry for doubting you and for ruining our night."

"Yeah? Well, I'm sorry you did, too." Tripp hopped out of the truck, walked around it and opened the passenger door, helping Dee down.

Dionna looked stunned. But his bruised ego and battered feelings wouldn't permit him to give her a pass. Not yet.

He closed the passenger door, and they walked toward the house. "By the way, I didn't get to tell you how incredible you look tonight."

"Thanks," she practically whispered as she followed him into the kitchen. She hung by the door, as if she suddenly felt out of place in the space she'd called home for most of her time in Royal. "If you'd prefer that I take my things and check into The Bellamy, I'd understand."

"For God's sake, Dee. I'm not tossing you out. I'm pissed and disappointed and maybe a little hurt because I would never have presumed the worst of you." Tripp rubbed his forehead and winced, his temples throbbing. "I'm gonna turn in early. I promised to help Jay with a small project out at his place tomorrow morning. I'll be gone before breakfast, but I should be home in time for dinner." He dropped a hurried kiss on her forehead. "Good night."

Tripp walked away, then halted at the bottom of the stairs. "Apology accepted."

He trotted up the steps, stripped out of his clothing and got ready for bed. But he couldn't go to sleep because his bed felt colder, emptier and a hell of a lot lonelier without Dionna Reed in it.

After several nights of the best sleep of her life in Tripp's arms, Dee awakened frazzled and exhausted.

She'd spent the entire night tossing and turning. Seeing the hurt and disappointment in Tripp's eyes over and over again. Hearing the pain in his voice. And she'd felt exactly like the ass she'd been to him.

Tripp had begrudgingly accepted her apology. But he hadn't said he'd forgiven her or that he'd been willing to put the incident behind them. She couldn't blame him. Every awful word she'd said to him had been burned into her brain and played over and over on a loop.

If she couldn't forgive herself, why should he?

Their tryst had been fun while it'd lasted. But she'd proven to be more trouble than she was worth.

He'd probably wanted to toss her out on her ass last night but had refrained from doing so for Ex and Ari's sake. Hadn't this been Xavier's concern all along? That if the two of them got involved, things would spin out of control and then cause excruciating tension that would ruin their wedding?

Ex had been right. They'd been playing with fire.

Dee's phone rang and she quickly picked it up, hoping it was Tripp calling to check in, as he often did throughout the day while working on the ranch.

It wasn't; it was Ari.

"Hey." Dee tried to muster a smile. "How are you, hon?"

"What's wrong?" Ariana's voice was fraught with alarm. "Did something happen with the wedding plans?"

"No. Everything is fine with the wedding plans." Dee sank onto the desk chair in her suite.

"Then this is about you and Tripp," Ari said matter-of-factly. "What happened? Did you two have a fight?"

Dee's face was hot. Despite Ari's teasing about her and Tripp, she hadn't told her friend what had happened between them. Yet, she instinctively seemed to know. And Dee was too hurt and exhausted to deny the truth about them anymore.

Dionna's eyes burned as tears spilled down her cheeks. "This was a mistake… I shouldn't have come to Tripp's ranch. And I should never have…" She sniffled, unable to say the words. "I should leave."

"Did Tripp do something to make you uncomfortable?" Ariana asked.

"No, it's nothing like that. I'm the one who screwed up and now…" Dee pressed a hand to her mouth to muffle her quiet sob. "I let what happened with my ex get in my head, and I was awful to Tripp when he's been nothing but sweet. What I said… I think it really hurt him."

"Did you apologize?"

"Of course!"

"Did Tripp ask you to leave?" Ariana asked.

"He's too much of a gentleman for that," Dee said with a sad smile. "He wouldn't, even if he wanted me to."

"People make mistakes, Dee. And couples have arguments. That doesn't mean—"

"We aren't a couple, and we never will be. In a few days, I'm returning home and he'll be…here." Dee dragged a hand across her face, glad she hadn't bothered to put on any makeup. "Maybe it's better if we just cut the cord now. Maybe it's cleaner this way. Less painful."

"It doesn't sound less painful for either of you," Ari noted.

Dee smoothed her hair back and sighed. "I tried to convince myself I could have this little meaningless fling and then just walk away. I didn't expect to feel so…*connected*, you know?"

"To Tripp?"

"And to Royal," Dee confessed. "I never imagined that I'd actually enjoy being here. That this was a place I could see myself living."

"Wow." Ariana's declaration was followed by a few moments of silence between them. "I guess neither of us saw that coming."

"No, I guess we didn't. Which is why getting involved with Tripp was a mistake."

"Dee, you don't actually believe that, and you know it," Ari said. Suddenly, there were sounds around her, like she was in a public space. "You're both just hurt, and the relationship feels untenable, so maybe you're both trying to retreat as a way to protect your hearts."

"What did Tripp do?" Xavier's voice was in the background.

"Nothing, sweetie. Your cousin has been a perfect gentleman, just like he promised. Settle down." Ari's response was followed by the sound of a kiss.

"Did Xavier join you on the set in Peru?" Dee asked.

"Actually, he just met me at JFK. We'll be boarding our flight to Dallas in a couple of hours. So sit tight and don't do anything until I get there. Everything is going to be fine, honey. I promise."

"Okay." Dee sucked in a deep breath and nodded. "Do you want me to pick you two up at the airport?"

"No, we're going to rent a car. And we're staying with Ex's parents. They'll be back from their trip to Cuba later tonight. And Tripp's sister is throwing an impromptu party for us tomorrow," Ari said. "I guess Tripp didn't tell you."

"No, he didn't." Dee's shoulders sagged and her stomach knotted. "Clearly, Tripp hasn't forgiven me. I honestly can't blame him for that."

"Dee, sweetie, you don't always have to be perfect, you know. None of us are. And I will love you to the moon and back…no matter what. Whether you're in LA, Paris or right there in Royal. I will always be your biggest fan, and I will always support whatever it is you want to do. You know that, right?"

"Same," Dee said. "Now don't miss your plane. I'll see you when you get here."

Dionna ended the call and sighed softly, unsure of

how her final days in Royal would turn out. But regardless of how things ended between her and Tripp, she hoped they could walk away as friends. Because she'd much rather have Tripp as a friend than to not have him in her life at all.

Fifteen

Tripp leaned against the doorway of the great room at his sister and Ryan's place, Bateman Ranch, with an ice-cold bottle of beer in his hand. As soon as Tripp had alerted Tessa that Ex and Ari would be popping into town for a few days, his sister had hastily planned this little afternoon party of around fifty people.

The sun had set, and the crowd had thinned out. Tripp's parents had returned from their three-week trip to Cuba. His mother had spent most of the party catching up on lost time with her beloved grandchildren and playing twenty questions with Dionna, under the guise of getting to know her. Which made him wonder *exactly* what Tess had told their mother about him and Dee.

His dad had given him a knowing look and chuckled.

But an hour ago, his parents had taken the kids back to their little ranch house to spend the night with Grandma and Grandpa. Tessa and Ryan looked like they'd won the lottery and probably couldn't wait until everyone left so they could get some adult time in without the kids.

Tripp was glad that Ariana seemed to get on well with his aunt and uncle, who both really seemed to appreciate her moving the wedding to Royal. And even though he and Dee hadn't spoken much since the night of the mixer, he was glad to see how well she got along with his family. Especially his mother who'd given him what he could only describe as a nod of approval just before she and his dad had practically kidnapped his niece and nephew.

Tripp bumped fists with his friend Jay Chatman as Jay headed out. He was surprised by the sudden voice behind him.

"I like her. A lot," Audra Covington said.

He didn't need to ask whom she was referring to. He'd been staring at Dee again and now Audra was, too.

Audra was a celebrity-status jewelry designer who'd made Royal her part-time home, along with her husband, Darius Taylor-Pratt, who was the owner of a quickly growing athletic clothing company, Thr3d, and an heir to the fortune left by late billionaire Buckley Blackwood. Something Darius hadn't known most of his life. Tripp, Tessa and Ryan had befriended Audra when she'd come to town to work on a commission by another one of the Blackwood heirs. They'd first met while working together on a volunteer landscaping project at the Texas Cattleman's Club.

"Dee? Yeah, she's great. She and Ariana go way back to middle school," Tripp said.

"You know what I mean." Audra propped a hand on her hip, which only accentuated her pregnant belly.

"No, I don't." Tripp finished the last of his beer and feigned innocence.

"Look, I know you didn't ask for my advice, and if you don't want it, feel free to tell me to shut the hell up." Audra repeated the same words Tripp had uttered to her three years earlier.

Tripp couldn't help chuckling. He tossed the empty bottle in a nearby recycling bin, then turned to Audra, his arms folded. "Okay, Mama Bear. Shoot. Let's hear these words of wisdom you have for me."

"Be honest with her and with yourself. Whatever you're feeling, just…feel it. Don't pretend the feelings aren't there. Wade through them, rather than trying to find a way around them. That'll only get you stuck in the quicksand. If you don't tackle your emotions head-on, they'll sabotage any future relationships you have," Audra said.

Tripp shook his head and chuckled. He rubbed his bearded chin. "You realize you pretty much said *verbatim* what I told you when you and Darius were at your little crossroads three years ago?"

"I do." Audra grinned proudly as she stretched her back and rubbed her belly. "What you said that day was a turning point for me in my relationship with Darius. If it hadn't been for your unsolicited advice, who knows? Dare and I might never have come to terms with our feelings for each other. Your advice was life-changing for me, Tripp. That's why I never forgot it. Seems you could use a little of your own advice where Dionna is concerned."

Tripp leaned against the doorway again and frowned. He shoved one hand in his pocket. "The situation is different with me and Dee. I'm here and she lives in LA."

"Did you forget why Darius and I have two homes and split our time between Royal and LA?" Audra laughed. She caught her husband's gaze as he stood on the other side of the room chatting with Ryan. Darius winked at her and she blew a kiss at him.

Tripp wasn't jealous of their relationship at all. *Really.*

"I didn't forget," Tripp said. "And I'm glad you two were able to make it work. But it was different with you. You and Darius had been in a relationship before. You were simply rekindling the feelings you already had for each other."

"Don't downplay your intuition when it comes to Dee. If you think there's something special between you two, don't be afraid to tell her so."

Tripp glanced up at Dee again. He rubbed the back of his neck. "Thanks, Audra. That honestly does help."

"I'm rooting for you both." Audra grinned, then handed him her empty bottle of sparkling water. "Now I'm headed to the restroom again because our child really seems to enjoy bouncing on my bladder."

Tripp laughed then chucked the bottle into the recycling bin. Maybe Audra was right. He and Dionna weren't twentysomethings who were still discovering themselves. They both knew what they wanted in life. Maybe they both knew *who* they wanted, too.

But he couldn't just up and leave the ranch for months at a time the way Darius and Audra were able to. It wouldn't be fair to put such a burden on Tessa who already had her hands full raising a family. But it wouldn't be fair of him to expect Dee to be the only one to make sacrifices so they could be together either.

He'd looked at the situation a dozen different ways, and it just felt hopeless.

Right person. Wrong situation.

"Hey, Tripp." Ari stood beside him. "I wanted to thank you again for everything you've done for Xavier and me. But most of all, I want to thank you for taking such good care of my best friend. She adores you, you know."

"I feel the same way about her," Tripp admitted. He'd been hurt and angry because he cared for Dee so much. That hadn't changed.

"Then don't let a stupid argument ruin the time you have left together." Ari's expression was the most serious he'd ever seen it.

"That's the thing." Tripp's brows furrowed. "No matter what, in a few days she'll be boarding that plane back to Hollywood. Then what?"

Ari slipped her arm through his and smiled as they both glanced over at Dee who was talking to

Xavier and his parents. "That, Tripp Noble, is up to the two of you."

Tripp turned to her, confused. "Dee is your right hand at the studio."

"And in case the two of you haven't noticed, she's been running things from here just fine. In fact, she hasn't skipped a beat. When she's needed to travel, she has." Ari grinned. "Don't make this more complicated than it needs to be."

"And you'd go for that? If she wanted to make Royal her base of operations long-term?"

"Would it be the most ideal situation? No," Ari admitted. "But Dionna is first and foremost my best friend. I want her to be happy. And it seems to me that she's been pretty happy here in Royal with you." Ari squeezed his shoulder, then returned to the sofa where she snuggled up beside Xavier.

Nope. He wasn't jealous of their relationship either. Or at least that's the story his brain was trying to sell his heart. But it seemed neither of them were buying it.

Who was he kidding? The time he'd spent with Dionna made him see that was exactly what he wanted. He'd watched Dee with Dylan and Tiana, and he couldn't help wondering what *their* kids might look like.

Tripp's mind was running at a million miles an hour with all the things he wanted to say to Dee. But first, there was something he needed to do.

Dionna returned to The Noble Spur with a bag filled with leftovers from the party. She carefully removed each dish Tessa had packed for her and Tripp from the cloth bag and stored it in the refrigerator.

Tripp had suddenly left the party, asking Ex if he wouldn't mind dropping Dee at the ranch. He'd barely spoken to her since *accepting* her apology. And since Ari and Ex's unexpected visit, they'd been busy showing the couple the plans for the wedding or game planning with Rylee Meadows about how they should handle the infamous wedding crasher, Patrick MacArthur, who'd apparently set his sights on disrupting Ariana and Xavier's wedding.

Headlights flashed through the kitchen window, indicating Tripp had returned to the ranch. Dionna's first instinct was to turn out the kitchen lights and hurry up the stairs to her suite. To continue giving Tripp the space he seemed to need. But in a few more days, she'd be leaving.

Dee couldn't help thinking about her conversation with Ari. About people making mistakes and couples having arguments. Maybe what she and Tripp had was destined to be short-lived. That didn't negate how momentous their time together had been… For her, at least. So she'd never forgive herself if she didn't do everything in her power to ensure they both had fond memories of the time they'd spent together.

Tripp stepped into the kitchen and closed the door behind him. He seemed surprised to see her there.

"Hey." He shoved a hand in his pocket and leaned against the counter. "I figured you and Ariana would be out somewhere painting the town. She was a little—"

"High-strung tonight?" Dionna smiled, wrapping

her arms around herself. "Yeah, she was. She's so happy to be off set and to be with Xavier again and—"

"And her best friend." A small smile lit his eyes. "She obviously missed you. I thought she was going to squeeze you to death when she first saw you."

"It was a distinct possibility." Dee's eyes stung with unshed tears despite her smile, and her stomach was tied in knots. She swallowed hard and took a few steps toward Tripp, her heart racing. "Tripp, about the other night… I am really, *really* sorry. I wish I could go back and—"

"I know." Tripp took a few steps forward. "Me too."

"You don't have any reason to apologize." She inched closer still, her eyes locked with his.

"Given what you've been through and what you saw… I understand why you were upset." He gathered a few of her loose twists, running his fingers through them. "I overreacted. I sort of flashed back to a past relationship of my own."

"I've missed you so much." Dee wrapped her arms around him, fisting the back of his shirt. Her voice trembled slightly.

"It was just two days, and the entire time, you were right down the hall. But…" Tripp cradled her face. "It felt like so much longer. What am I gonna do when you're two thousand miles away?" His voice grew quiet, and he sighed.

"That's what I've been asking myself these past few days," Dee whispered. She blinked back tears. "But I don't want to think about that anymore. I just want us to have the most amazing time together for the next few—"

Suddenly, Tripp's mouth was on hers. His tongue parted her lips and glided along hers. She was overwhelmed with a deep sense of joy, thankful they'd made up and that he was kissing her again. Setting her skin on fire and causing a steady pulsing between her thighs from his kiss and touch alone.

Her eyes brimmed with fat tears that spilled down her cheeks.

Tripp kissed her tear-stained cheek. Then he slipped the off-shoulder sweater over her head and dropped it on the floor. He unbuttoned her jeans, slid them down her hips and carried her to the sofa. Then he pulled the large cashmere throw over them and lay atop her. Dionna tugged his Henley shirt and the T-shirt he wore beneath it over his head. She dropped them to the floor. When she reached for the button of Tripp's pants, he stopped her.

"The condoms are upstairs," he practically growled between kisses to her neck and bare shoulder. "I'm not feeling the strongest sense of control right now. So maybe we'd better play it safe and—"

"Keep the python in its cage?" Dee pressed a hand to the clearly visible outline of his erection pressed against the fabric of his pants.

Tripp shuddered visibly, and in that moment, she'd felt incredibly powerful.

"Something like that." Tripp grinned. "Besides, I'm not gonna need a condom for what I have in mind."

Tripp's brown eyes twinkled, and before Dee could speak, his head had disappeared beneath the cashmere throw. He spread her legs wide, to accommodate the width of his shoulders, and tugged aside the soaked fabric shielding her sex.

Dee gripped his shoulders, moaning with pleasure at the delicious sensation of his tongue against her most sensitive flesh. Lips pressed together, Dee tried to hold back all of the involuntary sounds of satisfaction trying to escape her throat. It was a lost cause.

Her head lolled back against the pillow, and her eyes wrenched shut as her soft murmurs became more vocal, followed by a few choice curse words, and perhaps some begging. And when Tripp had pushed his fingers inside her, stroking the space that always drove her wild with desire, and sucked on her sensitive clit, she'd fallen apart. Her fingers in his hair and his name on her tongue, she shattered, her chest heaving and her eyes clouding with tears.

She wanted to savor this moment between them, and every other moment they'd get to share over the next few days. But all she could think about was that this was one of the last times she'd be with him, and it broke her heart.

Tripp pressed a kiss to her damp cheek. "You okay, sweetheart?"

She nodded, wiping at her wet eyes and probably making an absolute mess of her makeup. But at this point, she didn't care.

Since they'd been housemates, Tripp had seen her in various states of undress, with and without her makeup. Her hair a mess. Her sleeping in her bonnet. And it had never once changed the way he'd looked at her. The only thing he hadn't witnessed was her on her knees. Something she honestly hadn't ever been very fond of. But for him… She wanted to give him this. For Tripp to understand how deeply she felt for him, even if she couldn't make herself say the words.

"Ready to go upstairs?" he asked.

Dee shook her head. She squirmed from beneath him and stood. "I want you sitting right here."

When she sank to her knees, he seemed surprised. Tripp tipped her chin. "You know that's not why I do that, right? That I get off on it as much as you do?"

Dee nodded, but she unfastened and unzipped his pants just the same. Then she looked up at him and smiled. "And this is something I really want to do for you."

Tripp's chest heaved as he watched Dee grip the base of his length and take him inside her mouth until she gagged a little before backing off a bit. He groaned at the intense pleasure of her warm mouth gliding up and down his already painfully erect dick.

She started off slow and tentative. But with each murmur of pleasure and each curse he uttered, she seemed to gain more confidence. To relish the power she had over him.

Tripp lightly gathered her hair, which had fallen forward, in his fist, not wanting to miss a moment of his length gliding in and out of that pretty little mouth. The erotic scene escalated the incredible sensation crawling up his spine, making his head feel lighter with each breath he took.

He fought the urge to move his hips. He was already so close, and he wanted to make this unexpected moment between them last as long as he possibly could.

But when Dee added the twisting of her hand as her mouth glided up and down his dick, he was at his breaking point.

"Fuck, Dee. If you don't stop now, I'm gonna…"

A wicked glint lit Dee's dark eyes as she intensified her efforts. She understood his warning, but she had no intention of backing off. She sucked harder and faster, her jaws hollowing and her hands working him until he'd lost complete control, his body emptying into hers.

Tripp collapsed against the sofa, his chest heaving and his pulse racing as he pulled Dionna into his arms, settling her onto his lap. He kissed her shoulder, her neck, her jaw. Then he pressed his mouth to hers.

"I love you, Dionna Reed." He whispered the words into her ear before pressing another kiss there. But instead of his declaration making her happy, she buried her face in his neck, her warm tears wetting his skin.

Dee hadn't responded in-kind to his spontaneous utterance. And maybe he didn't have the right to expect her to after their short time together. Still, she obviously felt something for him, too.

That would have to be enough for now.

Tripp lay in his bed in his darkened room, with Dee's cheek pressed to his bare chest. He'd come to love holding Dee in his arms like this after they'd made love. He cherished the comfort of her warm, soft body molded to his. The way her dark hair spread out over his chest. The soft sighs she made in her sleep. The tickle of her warm breath skittering across his skin.

But tonight, his brain couldn't stop reminding him that every moment with Dee would be one of their last.

It'd never bothered him before. Every relationship had an expiration date. Like a gallon of milk or a block of cheese. He'd been grateful for the memories, edified by the lessons and ready to move on. But the thought of moving on from Dee… It felt like someone had carved a hole in his chest and was pulling his heart out.

He didn't want to move on from Dionna. He wanted her in his life. Wanted to keep waking up to her each morning and falling asleep with her in his arms each night.

This didn't feel like the end. It felt like the beginning of his future. A future that revolved around Dionna Reed. He was devastated by the thought of losing her.

Tripp glided a hand up and down the soft skin of Dee's bare back. He kissed the top of her head.

"Mmm…" She pressed a kiss to his chest. "You hungry? Your sister loaded us up with leftovers."

"I'm good." He tucked her head beneath his chin. "The only thing I'm hungry for is you."

Dee giggled and kissed his chest again, her hand planted dangerously low on his belly.

"After we just made up for those two days apart

and a lot more?" she teased, sitting up in bed and pulling the sheet up to cover her bare breasts. "I'd think you'd be exhausted by now."

He was. But that hadn't abated his desire for her in the least. He was already partially erect and thinking of positions they had yet to try. "I'll catch up on my sleep once you're gone."

Dee frowned and her shoulders tensed. "I should get ready for bed."

She climbed out of bed, then dipped into the bathroom. When she returned, she was wearing one of his T-shirts emblazoned with The Noble Spur brand, and her hair was neatly secured beneath her bonnet. She nuzzled her face into his shoulder and settled in to go to sleep.

"Dee, have you considered *not* returning to LA?" Could she hear the erratic thumping of his heart as he finally managed to ask the question that'd been brewing in his head since his conversation with Ariana.

The muscles of her back tensed beneath his fingertips, and she didn't speak right away. He knew Dee well enough to know she was measuring her response. Trying not to say the first thing that popped into her head.

"Of course, I've thought about it," Dee said finally. "But we both know that isn't an option, Tripp. My life is there and yours is here."

The aching silence between them lingered, as if time itself had slowed.

"What if you could keep working from here...like

you've been doing? And then traveling whenever it's required?" he asked.

"Ari would never go for that." Dee lifted onto one elbow, her gaze searching his in the dim bedroom light filtering through the curtains.

"But what if she would? Would you consider it?" He stroked her cheek.

Dee swallowed hard. The pained expression in her eyes provided her answer before she opened her mouth. "Tripp, what's happened between us has been incredible. We've fallen so hard and so fast that…it scares me."

"Why?" He sat up, too. The question came out sounding too desperate, and he did his best to reel it back, not wanting to pressure her. "I mean… I honestly haven't felt like this about anyone else. I can't imagine not holding you every night. Not making breakfast with you in the morning. And I'm pretty sure Deuce believes he's your horse now instead of mine." He swallowed hard and took her hand in his. "Am I really the only one who feels like this is just the beginning of something special?"

"No," Dee whispered. "I feel that, too. Every day. But what if we're wrong? What if this feels so amazing because it's new? Because other than my screwup the other night, this hasn't really been tested?"

"Then we'll work it out. Just like we did tonight." Tripp squeezed her hand.

"What if we can't? Leaving LA where my family and friends are… Maybe changing my career… It's a big ask, Tripp. It's thrilling, but also terrifying.

I want to stay, believe me. But… I can't. I'm sorry."
She sniffled.

Tripp winced, his head spinning and his chest aching. "It's okay, baby. I understand."

He pulled Dee into his arms, and she settled against his chest again. He kissed her temple, then propped one arm behind his head as he stared at the ceiling in his darkened room.

He'd made his big ask, and Dee had turned him down. Tripp was disappointed, but he understood her reluctance when she was the only one making a sacrifice.

But he had one more card left to play.

Sixteen

Dee zipped the last of her luggage closed and handed it to Roy Jensen, who had been patiently waiting for her while she stalled in packing the last of her things.

She and Tripp had spent nearly every moment possible together over the past few days. And when they'd gone to dinner at The Royal Diner, The Eatery or The Silver Saddle, they'd held hands and he'd kissed her. And she hadn't cared who'd seen them together.

They'd spent time with Tripp's family and the new friends she'd made in town, and she'd never felt more at ease. Every day it got harder, knowing she'd have to board her plane today.

So she'd been surprised to wake up and discover Tripp gone. He'd yet to return to the ranch, though he'd known she'd be leaving soon. She'd been stalling, hoping he'd come back in time to say goodbye. But maybe avoiding a painful goodbye was best.

Wouldn't she prefer to remember all the wonderful moments they'd shared instead of making her last memory of Tripp her blubbering like a lovelorn fool?

"Ready, Miss Dee?" Roy asked for the fourth or fifth time. "I hate to rush you, but I've got to make a quick stop before we hit the road."

"Of course. Thank you for being so patient, Roy. We'd better go."

"Yes, ma'am." Roy placed his Stetson back on his head and gathered up the last of her luggage.

As she rode in the truck with Roy, Dee was determined not to cry again. She'd shed enough tears, and it hadn't changed anything. She was still leaving Royal, and she was brokenhearted over it. As devastated as she was about walking away from Tripp, it pained her to leave behind the town of Royal that had truly begun to feel like home these past few weeks. And the people whom she'd come to regard as friends and family. But she couldn't help feeling as if she was betraying her own friends and family by thinking that way.

Roy pulled into the parking lot of the Texas Cattleman's Club and parked. "Sorry, ma'am. This won't take long. Promise. We'll still be able to get you to your flight in plenty of time."

"All right." Dee nodded, glancing out of the window as Roy climbed out the other side of the truck. She was stunned when the passenger door opened, and Tripp extended a hand to her. "Tripp, what are you doing here?"

"You didn't think I'd actually let you leave town without saying goodbye, did you?"

Dee forced a smile and shook her head. She gave Tripp her hand and he led her inside.

"You'll have plenty of time to catch that plane," Tripp said. "But I have something to show you."

They walked into the club and entered the space where Ariana and Xavier's reception would be held.

Dee stopped, both of her hands pressed to her mouth as she glanced around. The dimly lit space was decked out in fairy lights and candles.

"It's beautiful, Tripp." Dionna glanced around the room before turning back to him and cradling his stubbled cheek. "This was incredibly sweet of you. Thank you."

He looped his arms around her waist and tugged her closer. "I have a proposition, Dionna Reed… Stay with me."

"What?" She met his gaze. "Tripp, you know I can't—"

"Before you answer, there's someone you should talk to." Tripp pulled out his phone and handed it to her.

"Hello?" Dee's eyes didn't leave Tripp's.

"Hi, sweetie." It was Ariana. "I just need you to know that I appreciate what an amazing friend you are. That you've always been there to look after me. That's why there is nothing more important to me than seeing you happy. And there in Royal, with the man you love, you are the happiest I've ever seen you, Dee. So if you want to return to LA, do it because it's what you want. Not because you're worried about me or the company."

Dionna turned her back to Tripp as tears streaked down her face. "I appreciate what you're doing, but I love my work."

"Good. Because I love working with you. But, sweetie, we're in the age of technology. You've been working from Royal for the past few weeks and everything here is just fine. Yes, we'd have to rearrange the duties here a bit. Maybe bring on another staff member. But it would be worth it. So make your choice based on what you want, Dee. We'll work everything else out. Now, I think there's someone waiting for an answer from you. Either way, know that you have my full support. Love you."

"Love you, too." Dee ended the call and handed the phone back to Tripp. She wiped tears from her eyes with the back of her fingers. "You really want me to stay, huh?" She laughed nervously.

"I really, *really* do," he said. "And I realize it isn't fair for you to be the only one to make sacrifices in the relationship. So I've made a few arrangements."

"Like?" She studied his handsome face.

"The fee I'm being paid for the film… I'm using it to pay up your apartment lease for the next year. So if you ever decide this isn't what you want…you can always go back home. You already know your job will still be there."

"Tripp, that's very generous. But I can't ask you to do that."

"And you didn't. I need to show you I'm just as invested in this relationship as you are, Dionna." Tripp said. "I obviously can't transport the ranch, but I'd like to be able to travel with you sometimes. So I've given Roy a well-deserved promotion. He'll be taking on more responsibilities at the ranch, so the additional burden doesn't fall on Tess."

"Why are you willing to do all this for me, Tripp?" She leaned in closer, her hands pressed to his chest.

Tripp's eyes shone in the dim club as he wrapped his arms around her. "Because I am madly, deeply in love with you, Dionna Reed. You're beautiful inside and out. You're brilliant and funny, mostly when you're not trying," he chuckled. "You're truly special and you challenge me in all the right ways. With you, every day I feel like I'm becoming a better man. And I don't want to lose that. I don't want to lose you. Say you'll stay. *Please*."

Tears filled Dee's eyes and her heart felt so full it might burst. "I'd like to see you get rid of me now, Austin Charles Noble the third. Because I love you, and there's no place on earth I'd rather be than right here with you."

Tripp hugged her tight, lifting her from her feet momentarily before returning her to the turquoise-colored soles of her cowboy boot–clad feet. Yet, it felt as if she was floating. She honestly couldn't ever remember being happier.

Tripp pressed his lips to hers and kissed her, reminding her of the moments they'd shared and how much she adored him. But when they pulled out of their kiss and opened their eyes, the room was pitch-black, except for the flickering candles on the table.

"What happened?" she asked.

"It's not just the club. Looks like we got ourselves a town-wide blackout." She recognized Roy Jensen's voice. "That means we might run into traffic. So if we're still headed to the airport, I reckon we better head on out."

Tripp looked at Dee and she grinned.

"No, sir. I'm not going anywhere. I plan to stay right here."

"Yes, ma'am." Roy seemed pleased. "Then I'll return your bags to the ranch and I guess I'll see you two there later." He turned and left.

"I hope you don't take this blackout as a sign of bad luck." Tripp nuzzled her neck, his beard tickling her skin.

"We don't need luck," Dee said. "We have love."

Tripp stared at the gorgeous woman who'd blown in like a tornado across the rolling plains of Texas and had stolen his heart. He kissed her again. "Yes, indeed, we do."

* * * * *

Who will the blackout bring together?
Find out in the next book,
Designs on a Rancher,
by LaQuette.

#2929 DESIGNS ON A RANCHER

Texas Cattleman's Club: The Wedding • by LaQuette

When big-city designer Keely Tucker is stranded with Jacob Chatman, the sexiest, most ambitious rancher in Texas, unbridled passion ignites. But will her own Hollywood career dreams be left in the rubble?

#2930 BREAKAWAY COWBOY

High Country Hawkes • by Barbara Dunlop

Rodeo cowboy Dallas Hawkes has an injured shoulder and a suspicious nature. Giving heartbroken Sierra Armstrong refuge at his ranch is a nonstarter. But the massage therapist's touch can help heal his damaged body. And open a world of burning desire in his lonely bed...

#2931 FRIENDS...WITH CONSEQUECES

Business and Babies • by Jules Bennett

The not-so-innocent night CEO Zane Westbrook spent with his brother's best friend, Nora Monroe, was supposed to remain a secret. But their temporary fling turns permanent when she reveals she's expecting Zane's baby!

#2932 AFTER THE LIGHTS GO DOWN

by Donna Hill

It's lights, camera, *scandal* when competing morning-show news anchors Layne Davis and Paul Waverly set their sights on their next career goals. Especially as their ambitions and attraction collide on set...and seductive sparks explode behind closed doors!

#2933 ONE NIGHT WAGER

The Gilbert Curse • by Katherine Garbera

When feisty small-town Indy Belmont takes on bad boy celebrity chef Conrad Gilbert in a local cook-off, neither expects a red-hot attraction. Winning a weekend in his strong, sexy arms may be prize enough! But only if Indy can tame her headstrong beast...

#2934 BIG EASY SECRET

Bad Billionaires • by Kira Sinclair

Jameson Neally and Kinley Sullivan are two of the best computer hackers in the world. Cracking code is easy. But cracking the walls around their guarded hearts? Impossible! When the two team up on a steamy game of cat and mouse, will they catch their culprit...or each other?

Get 4 FREE REWARDS!

We'll send you 2 FREE Books plus 2 FREE Mystery Gifts.

FREE Value Over **$20**

Both the **Harlequin® Desire** and **Harlequin Presents®** series feature compelling novels filled with passion, sensuality and intriguing scandals.

HARLEQUIN
PLUS

Announcing a **BRAND-NEW**
multimedia subscription service
for romance fans like you!

Read, Watch and Play.

Experience the easiest way to get
the romance content you crave.

Start your **FREE 7 DAY TRIAL** at
<u>www.harlequinplus.com/freetrial</u>.